Tales from the Fayrewood

by Verwood u3a Writers Circle

All rights reserved. No part of this book may be reproduced or transmitted by any means; electronic, mechanical, photocopying or otherwise without the prior permission of the copyright holder.

Primary author: Alan Pearce

Contributors: Viv Gough, Helen Griffith, Ted Mason, Jan Mills, Barbara Shea, Lesley Watts, Tony Wilson, Carol Waterkeyn

Compiled and edited by Alan Pearce

Cover photo: Helen Griffith

ISBN 9798325235092

Verwood u3a Writers Circle
A compendium of our work
Introduction by the Group Leader

The Verwood University of the Third Age Writers Circle was inaugurated in 2022 as part of the expansion of Verwood u3a generally. Verwood u3a must be one of the most successful and expanding u3as in the UK under a recent succession of go-ahead committees and Chairs. Its website is nothing short of stupendous. The Writers Circle is proud to be a part of it all.

I am Alan Pearce, founder and leader of the group. We started with six members, which rapidly grew to eight and then remained steady at five for a while. Then in 2023 two new members joined out of nowhere (well, out of China and Hong Kong actually) and then at the 2023 Open Day we picked up three more new members. People have tended either to go, or to remain fiercely loyal and as I write we are stable at ten members, which must remain a maximum.

At each meeting, we read our pieces on a subject set by consensus at the previous meeting – maximum 800 words; then for the second half of the meeting it is Open House for anything whatsoever to do with creative writing or creative thinking – the possibilities are seemingly endless and have resulted in much mirth and enjoyment.

Three members have already published books, and since formation we have had articles published in local magazines, had multiple readings on Forest FM community radio and had several letters published in national newspapers and in *Daily Telegraph* books. It is now time to produce our own book – this compendium of our work, edited by me, the Group Leader.

At inception, I thought I would group the stories and articles into sections, with a topic heading which would effectively be a chapter heading. But this is not how our group works, such compartmentalisation; right from the very beginning we were all astonished how a single, simple topic such as "Retribution" or "Perspective" or "Time and Space" would always be interpreted in as many different ways as there were people present. For example, the set topic "Astonishment" brought forth from seven people: an affair that wasn't and a divorce that wasn't, a (defeated) gang war story, a Verwood cob house haunting incident, someone who lost their sense of smell, a Winchester market description, skulduggery in Russia and a descriptive piece about Route 40, Arizona. Such is the nature of the beast.

So instead, I decided simply to produce the works in absolutely no order at all but just to put at the top of each the genre, the set topic and the author's name. This means that you can delve into this tome anywhere you want, and it won't make any difference (except for the riddle) so you can simply enjoy the offerings as you will. Some are hilarious, some are sad, some are informative, some are just intriguing, several come from personal experiences and many, many have twists in the tail. I'm sure you, too, will be "astonished" at the very wide variety of articles which follow. This is a book for everyone.

It is important to stress that all entries remain the copyright and the responsibility of the author. It is also important to give thanks to all the contributors and particularly to Carol Waterkeyn additionally for her astonishing tenacity and superb work in formatting all of this and to Jan Mills for proofreading it. It could not have been done without them. Thank you.

This compilation, therefore, is for our satisfaction and readers' pleasure. Enjoy.

**Alan Pearce, Verwood,
June 2024**

The Contributors

Barbara Shea

Barbara was born in Blackpool, Lancashire and has lived in Verwood for thirty-nine years. Barbara left Blackpool when she was twenty-one. She and a friend wanted to see parts of the world they had never visited before, and they decided on Rhodesia (now Zimbabwe) as her friend had family there.

Barbara stayed and worked there for two years and it was where she met her late husband. They then spent three years in South Africa before returning to England and starting their family.

Barbara worked in and around Verwood for many years, her last job being with Mencap. Once retired and ever keen to travel, Barbara and her husband decided to backpack around the world and spent thirteen months travelling to various countries. Back in England, they decided to do it all again and two years later did another round the world trip with trusty backpacks, returning six months later following the birth of their first grandchild.

Barbara now volunteers for the National Trust and is interested in walking and painting, but has always been a keen writer and on joining the u3a

Writers group over a year ago, has written many short stories and is thoroughly enjoying the experience.

Barbara still lives in Verwood and has two children and two grandchildren.

Ted Mason

Ted was born in Bolivia to British parents. He moved to Bournemouth when he was only six months old. After college and university, he taught English literature and creative writing in a school in South Lincolnshire before moving back to teach in Dorset. He then spent seven years in central China working as an educational management advisor.

He has published two books; one about exploits in China, and the other is a collection of amusing short stories for children based on his experiences as a teacher. While in China he also wrote articles for the China Daily Newspaper, travelling throughout that vast and beautiful country. Following illness, he returned to Dorset to set up home in Verwood.

Now retired and single, with two children and four grandchildren, he still finds time to write and is involved in many u3a activities. His main interest is in folk music, performing in several clubs in Dorset.

Alan Pearce

Alan was born in Lancashire and educated at Bolton. Then after four years' training at the Britannia Royal Naval College in Dartmouth, he joined the Fleet in Singapore. He saw Eastern life from Kamchatka to the Antarctic, from the Philippines to the Indian ocean.

After a fairly torrid time in peacekeeping and other operations around the rest of the world, he took part in the Falklands Campaign and the Gulf War. In the meanwhile, he qualified as a Russian interpreter and had many adventures – some tragic, some hilarious, and all chronicled in his autobiography *How I dropped in on Vladimir Putin* (AmazonUK books).

On leaving the RN in 1996 he worked for twelve years at Cranborne Chase Communities, an organisation for young adults with learning disabilities, then for the charities AgeUK and HelpandCare before finally retiring – to take up a post with Citizens Advice, which he still holds.

Firmly ensconced with his wife in Verwood and u3a, he has three adult offspring and five grand offspring. His hobbies are writing, classical music, sea fishing, international affairs, country pursuits, poetry, Old Time Music Hall, gardening, linguistics, and bunking and debunking.

Tony Wilson

Tony was born just to the north of Hampton Court Palace in 1953.

After a couple of jobs after leaving school, Tony trained as an optician and qualified in 1976.

Writing has always been an interest; especially poetry, but so far worldwide fame has eluded him. He is also keen on history, puzzles, disco dancing and watching movies. At the age of nearly 40, Tony first trod the boards and over the years appeared in many, many plays, musicals and pantos. He also loves wine and chocolate.

Tony is married with three children and eight grandchildren so far!

Tony moved to Verwood three years ago and joined u3a soon after.

Carol Waterkeyn

Carol was originally from Southampton, relocated to Surrey for a number of years and moved to the Verwood area in 1993. A former civil servant and administrator, Carol also worked as BA cabin crew.

In her mid-30s Carol got the writing bug, and started penning articles for magazines. An opportunity arose to be assistant editor on a local publication, and soon after, editor. Subsequently she worked in PR and marketing, and joined a major UK charity as a writer and editor. After 10 years she became freelance for a few years before retiring.

In her spare time, Carol started writing her first children's book, *Magic in the Attic*, about 20 years ago and has written three more in the series since. She also writes short stories. She has recently published her first women's novel, *Casting Off*.

Over the years Carol has had a number of successes in writing competitions. She's had stories published in *The People's Friend*, *Mudeford Magazine*, *EGO Magazine* and two anthologies.

Carol joined the u3a Writers Circle in September 2023. She is married and has one grown-up daughter.

Jan Mills

Jan spent her whole working life supporting people with mental health needs and/or a learning disability. She worked in a range of roles across the NHS, Local Authority and Charity sectors. She retired in 2016 as CEO of a learning disability charity, a role she had held for twelve years.

Jan has always enjoyed English and other languages. She has a long-cherished ambition to write fiction or adapt classical fiction for people who may find reading a challenge. She would like to publish books with adult themes and concepts and make them accessible in plain English.

Jan is married with three adult children and two granddaughters. She lives in Verwood with her husband and a German Short-Haired Pointer.

Helen Griffith

Helen was born in Winchester and has lived in Verwood for three years.

Helen was brought up in High Wycombe, Buckinghamshire. She read German and English Literature at Warwick University before embarking on a career in software development. She took early retirement in September 2023.

Helen has lots of interests and hobbies including reading, puzzles and genealogy. She is a fully trained yoga teacher and is studying Ayurveda (encompassing lifestyle, food and medicine). She plays the piano, and acoustic and bass guitars. On retirement, Helen joined the Ramblers, Rest Less and u3a, where she is part of the gardening, history and writing groups. She joined the Writers Circle to see if she could write creatively, having only written technical documentation in the past.

Helen's love of nature led her and her devoted companion Poppy Poohsticks (Beagle) on many varied walks. She says Verwood is a lovely place to live with nature right on the doorstep and we are spoiled for choice if we go further afield.So, plenty of things to be involved in to avoid the housework!

Viv Gough

Viv was born in Northampton in 1946 and has lived in Verwood for twenty-three years.
    She was brought up in Pershore in Worcestershire and moved to Tenterden in Kent at the age of sixteen when her parents both changed jobs.
    She joined the Royal Air Force as a dental nurse at the age of eighteen and served at bases in Buckinghamshire and Gloucestershire before spending two years at RAF Changi in Singapore. She met her husband in the RAF and spent the following thirty years moving around England and the world, supporting his RAF and subsequent careers. She worked wherever she could, mainly in retail, and feels very lucky to have lived in many areas of the UK, as well as Cyprus, Kuwait and the UAE.
    Her interests include gardening, reading and theatre. Viv first joined a writing group in Kuwait and then another one seventeen years ago in West Moors. She has enjoyed writing mainly short stories in that time. She has won some competitions including the *Viewpoint magazine* short story competition twice. She would eventually like to see some of her writing in print for posterity.Viv is married with two children, three grandchildren and one great-grandchild.

Lesley Watts

Lesley was born in, and has lived in Dorset all her life, apart from four years residing in Wootton Bassett, Wiltshire, where she moved when first married – returning to Dorset and Verwood in 2000.

Her early career was as a secretary, moving to an accounts administrator role until deciding to pursue a long-held ambition by taking 'A' levels as a mature student, followed by a teaching degree at LSU in Southampton, qualifying in 1997. Lesley then taught across all year groups at Milldown Primary School in Blandford for 17 years, before leaving to explore other more leisurely pursuits.

Lesley's time is spent with family and friends, gardening, reading, watercolour painting, and nurturing her cats... as well as a love of walking and landscape/nature photography – which dovetail quite nicely. She also enjoys music and singing, and has recently taken up the ukulele.

Lesley has always loved creative writing, particularly free verse poetry: using words to create atmosphere and intrigue. So, joining u3a Writers Circle in 2022 has given her an artistic outlet to express and challenge herself in an environment which is both welcoming and supportive.

The u3a

The University of the Third Age (u3a) is an international movement whose aims are the education and stimulation of its mainly retired members. It started in France in 1973 at the Faculty of Social Sciences in Toulouse and came to the UK in 1981. It is voluntary: no-one is paid at any level, and it has a self-help ethos. It comprises both learning and activity groups. Verwood u3a has more than 30 different groups ranging from Art to the Writers Circle via investments, folk dance, jewellery making,guitar, bridge and badminton. The ethos of everything in u3a is "Learn,Laugh,Live."

The name is Verwood

It will not come as a surprise to readers to know that Verwood got its name from the Norman "Beau Bois" (1288). This became "Fair Wood" (1329) through "Fayrwood" (no letter 'e') (1438) to the present title, spurred by the Dorset Rolling Tongue and its exchange of the "F" for a "V".

Did you know there is another Verwood? Verwood, Saskatchewan, is seemingly miles from anywhere on the vast Canadian plains. It is 30 miles south of Old Wives Lake, a further 30 from Moose Jaw, 25 miles from the US border, and paradoxically just a horse ride from the Crane Valley! Saskatchewan itself, at 251,700 square miles, is almost exactly 5 times the size of England; its peak population has never been more than about one million.

Our Verwood grew from a population of 600 as a result of the railway spur on the Poole to Salisbury line, where they loaded the output of the brickworks and the potteries. Canada's Verwood arose out of the building of a huge grain silo on the Weyburn to Assiniboa part of the Canadian Pacific Railway, where they stored and then loaded wheat.

So, should we twin with them? Hardly. Because the similarity ends with the railway as well as beginning with it. Our Verwood has expanded considerably from a population of 600 (because the then Lord Cranborne seemingly said that he "wasn't having those new 'locomotive' things on their tracks coming snorting through my Cranborne land and frightening the cattle" so that the population followed the railway to Verwood).

Canada's Verwood has gone into decline and shrunk as a result of mechanisation to a total of just 15 people. It is now known as an "unincorporated community", having voted to downgrade from a "village" on 31st December 1954. It is virtually a ghost town. Most of its buildings are boarded up and only the grain elevator remains as a symbol of past importance.

While "our" Verwood was named from the French language how did Verwood, Canada get its name? Astonishingly, it was because the early dwellers decided they would name their settlement after the first person to die there – expecting it to be an elder of the settlement. Unfortunately, it was a six-year-old girl who tragically set her dress on fire as she stoked the stove to make a cup of tea for her father and died later from her burns. She was buried in the cemetery on the north side of Highway 13. Her name was Vera Wood.

But, to be clear, this tome is about Verwood, Dorset, UK!

Contents

Introduction		2
The contributors		4
About u3a		13
The name is Verwood		14
Barcelona	Barbara Shea	19
Emma	Tony Wilson	21
Electrical problems	Alan Pearce	23
Winchester Christmas...	Lesley Watts	25
Darkness and light	Carol Waterkeyn	27
Death in Australasia	Tony Wilson	29
Minor catastrophe	Helen Griffith	31
NI danger	Viv Gough	34
Divorce	Jan Mills	36
Armageddon	Ted Mason	39
Just Law	Lesley Watts	42
Eustace	Alan Pearce	44
The race	Ted Mason	45
Canyon	Tony Wilson	50
A dark story	Alan Pearce	51
A few limericks	Various	54
Goodbye to George	Viv Gough	55
Misunderstanding	Alan Pearce	57
Trousers	Ted Mason	59
Time to meditate	Helen Griffith	61
The obelisk	Tony Wilson	63
The good old days?	Jan Mills	64
Yan Men Pass	Ted Mason	67
Universal letter	Alan Pearce	70
Little Georgie Brown	Barbara Shea	72
The Airport	Jan Mills	74
Memories	Helen Griffith	76
Flash and microfiction	Various	78
The lost diary	Carol Waterkeyn	80
Snowman	Alan Pearce	83
Hearing	Barbara Shea	85
Crystal ball	Jan Mills	87
Space	Ted Mason	90

Arthur and Michael	Viv Gough	93
Girlfriends shock	Alan Pearce	96
Airport	Lesley Watts	98
Education as it is	Barbara Shea	99
The Master's apprentice	Tony Wilson	101
Oh, Dear!	Jan Mills	103
A hidden talent	Viv Gough	106
Clearly Curious ...	Alan Pearce	108
Memories	Ted Mason	110
AI	Barbara Shea	112
Witness value	Jan Mills	114
A walk	Lesley Watts	117
Holly's holly tree	Tony Wilson	119
Cheesemaking	Carol Waterkeyn	121
Social media	Alan Pearce	122
Grandma's cats	Barbara Shea	123
False prosecution?	Ted Mason	126
Henry and the Lobster	Tony Wilson	129
Cosmopolitan	Jan Mills	132
Slavs from Kostromo	Tony Wilson	135
Parking difficulties	Alan Pearce	137
Cocktails	Barbara Shea	140
The missing keys	Carol Waterkeyn	142
Richard and the ... lady	Tony Wilson	143
The Great u3a Debate	Anon	145
Train of thought	Helen Griffith	147
Put downs	Alan Pearce	150
Peevis smoking	Ted Mason	152
"When the cat's away"	Carol Waterkeyn	155
End of the collection	Viv Gough	158
"Earth"	Alan Pearce	160
Katie and Darren	Barbara Shea	162
A person of interest	Helen Griffith	164
Finding a hobby	Carol Waterkeyn	167
The Ship	Tony Wilson	170
Hubs	Ted Mason	171
The find	Viv Gough	174
Shouldn't have done it	Jan Mills	176

A deeply worrying story	Alan Pearce	179
Hiding in the wardrobe	Barbara Shea	182
Journey of self-discovery	Helen Griffith	184
Expensive date	Jan Mills	187
Mining on Triton	Tony Wilson	189
Discoveries	Alan Pearce	191
Fantastic space	Ted Mason	194
Striking gold	Carol Waterkeyn	196
Jet	Barbara Shea	198
A Blackpool day out	Carol Waterkeyn	201
Lines in the sand	Jan Mills	204
A line in the sand	Helen Griffith	206
Dolls and things	Viv Gough	207
Bournemouth in August	Tony Wilson	210
Serendipity	Alan Pearce	211
Nick's disengagement	Jan Mills	213
Sargent at the Tate	Lesley Watts	216
Moment of glory	Carol Waterkeyn	218
Coming back from France	Barbara Shea	221
The anniversary ...	Tony Wilson	224
Happy endings	Alan Pearce	226
Proper use of language	Anon	228

**The Writers Circle pieces.
They start now.
Enjoy!**

Genre: Fiction.Topic:"Retribution". By Barbara Shea

Barcelona

Ron sat alone on a bench, gazing at the crowds strolling down Las Ramblas. He'd always known he would love Barcelona. He'd wanted to come here for so long and finally, with the plane ticket his good friend George had given him, along with the two thousand euros in cash, here he was. He'd never have been able to afford a holiday like this himself had it not been for George. The five-star Alma Hotel was wonderful, the meals in the top restaurants had been a delight, and he was only sorry that his flight home was tomorrow.

He leaned back, closed his eyes, and let the sun warm his face. He felt, rather than saw, another person sitting next to him, and when he opened his eyes, he saw the most beautiful girl sitting further along the bench. She smiled at him, as she tossed her long black hair. He was mesmerised. She spoke to him in Spanish, and when he looked blank, she tried English. Her accent was charming, her skin glowing in the sunshine and her eyes large and dark. He was lost.

"Are you on holiday here?" she asked.

Ron replied that yes, he was on holiday, but had to return home the next day. She pulled a sad face, and at that moment a young man approached and spoke to her in Spanish. She replied and then said in

English: "This is my brother Alejandro, and my name is Valentina. It's Alejandro's birthday today, and we were just about to celebrate with a few drinks at a local bar. Would you like to join us?"

A moment of wariness washed over Ron, but Valentina smiled at him again and he found himself saying: "I'd be delighted".

With Valentina on one side and Alejandro on the other, they crossed Las Ramblas and set off down a dark alley. Ron's doubts resurfaced as they guided him into a dingy looking bar. The plaster on the walls was peeling, there were dirty plastic tables and chairs scattered around, and a grubby looking barman in a stained vest top asked them what they wanted to drink. Ron was uncertain but Alejandro ordered for them. By now, Ron had become increasingly nervous and, as the drinks kept coming, he downed one after another to try and quell his misgivings.

Valentina and Alejandro, who were both very talkative to begin with, gradually became quieter, then said they had to go. The greasy barman presented Ron with a whopping three-hundred-euro bill. Ron felt himself sobering up very quickly.

"Three hundred euros!" he exclaimed. "That's outrageous and I'm not paying it." Alejandro shrugged.

"You will have to pay," he said. "We have no money."

Ron considered protesting further and walking away, but out of the corner of his eye he saw three tough-looking men approaching, one of them carrying a baseball bat.

"Okay, I'll pay," he muttered, as he peeled three hundred euros from the wad of notes in his pocket. He handed them to the barman, who disappeared with Valentina and Alejandro into a back room, presumably to share out the money.

Ron knew he'd been conned and as he weaved his way back down the alley and onto Las Ramblas, he wished his last few hours in Barcelona hadn't been marred by such an unpleasant experience. However, the thought that the euro notes were fake cheered him up immensely and anyway, George could always print some more.

With a smug sense of satisfaction Ron phoned the Guardia Civil from the airport. Retribution!

Genre: Fiction. Topic: "Regret". By Tony Wilson

Emma

I met Emma when I began working at a holiday job during the summer of 1970.

She was tall, slim, full of life, with crazy, curly brown hair and deep chestnut eyes that invited you in. To say I was smitten from the word go would be an understatement. I was nearly seventeen and a little shy – especially around girls, having attended an all-boys school from the age of eleven. She on the contrary was without any repressions and nearly nineteen.

We were the youngest in the office and worked together doing administrative work, answering the phones, making the tea and so on, so we spent a lot of time together. She began flirting with me on the third day and I lapped it up, unable to respond except for a puppy dog smile and a nervous laugh. She spoke of an on/off boyfriend but I could not believe she didn't have legions of admirers, so why would she bother with a gauche schoolboy who had absolutely no experience with girls.

However, she persisted and slowly as the days passed, I became more relaxed in her company, more confident in my speech and manner. The first kiss took me by surprise, we were saying goodbye at close on business one Friday when I took the brave step of leaning in to kiss her on the cheek, but Emma turned her head and our lips met. The kiss was brief but all weekend, I could not stop thinking about it and was nervous when Monday morning came around. She greeted me with that disarming smile of hers and I instantly relaxed. It then became a ritual that we would kiss goodbye each evening.

The week before I was due to leave the job and go back to sixth form, the boss asked for a volunteer to work late to collate some information for some urgent business the next day. Both Emma and I offered; she said if we both worked the job would take half the time. The boss agreed and so we found ourselves alone together in the office, after work, the doors locked. I made us both a cup of coffee and we quickly got the work done. When we had finished, we sat and chatted, neither of us wanting to leave. She wore a very short sundress and had seated herself in front of me in a way that invited my eyes to appreciate her long, long, tanned legs. My hormones were racing and she knew it. She came over and sat on my lap, we kissed and then she seduced me.

The last couple of days before I left, we stole every opportunity to be alone together at work, when the final Friday evening came, I promised to come to see her in the office after school the during the following week. However, as it turned out schoolwork was full on and I regret that I did not manage to get to the office until the following Friday. I was greeted with the news that Emma had left for a new job, giving no notice and no forwarding address. I was devastated.

I never saw Emma again. My one big regret is that I never told her that I loved her.

Genre: Fact-based story. Topic: "Difficulty". By Alan Pearce

Electrical problems

I had a bit of a problem yesterday. The old fluorescent tube in the garage had gone and I discovered that (because technology had moved on from 1995) a replacement would be very expensive. LEDs were relatively cheap and so I had purchased one online.

I decided to remove the old fluorescent fitting and tube and replace it myself. After all, when I took the old bit down there would,(would there not?), be three wires coming out of the ceiling: red, black and brown/green. Easy peasy.

Vowing to remember which colour was which, I turned off the power and removed the old fitting. Aaagh! Ours was a modern house with multi-circuits and there were nine wires jutting from the ceiling, two of them going into a little plastic junction thing.

Careful, I thought. Just remember which three go into the old fluorescent unit. That's all you have to do. Simple. So, making a mental note of which were the three important wires I unscrewed the old unit. It came down quite easily and I turned to put it on the adjacent stepladder. When I turned back, I saw to my horror that all nine wires had sprung back into the ceiling cavity. I fished them out, stared at them, and swore gently. Which were those three important ones again?

With some trepidation I connected the three most likely ones to the new LED unit. I turned the power on at the mains and threw the garage light switch. Nothing. Stay calm, I thought, logic it out. The two black ones have got to be earth and the red ones live although I don't know why two of them should be connected. What can those green ones be? And the multicoloured ones?

At that moment my wife came out from the kitchen and said in a very matter-of-fact tone: "The lights have gone out in the kitchen!"

"Thank you, dear," I said. "I'll try and fix it."

I connected everything back the way it had been, or near enough, and went to check the kitchen. On the way out I absent-mindedly by habit flicked off the garage light. It came on.

"They're back on again!" came the cry from the kitchen. Oh! Good. Progress. But not there yet.

Hence, I thought: how many combinations are there with nine wires? Work it out then deduct the blacks and the connected reds. That got the combinations down to four figures. Hmm.

I thought the odds could be reduced because there was bound to be one red and one black. Although wrong, this gave me a clue and after an hour or so I got the garage light to come on. The only problem was that it wouldn't go off again. Another combination or two and I got it working. As I went to declaim my triumph to my sceptical wife, I noticed that I had left the outside security light on. I switched it off manually and went indoors.

"All the downstairs lights are now off," said my wife, laconically.

Back to the garage. Another couple of hours' work soon had the correct combination: garage light on/off – check; security light on/off – check. Downstairs lights (except for the utility room) on/off – check. Sicut satis. So now the only job remaining was to persuade my wife that we could easily do without a light in the utility room – it would save money, anyway, wouldn't it?

The flea in my ear impelled me to go back outside and re-contemplate the situation. After just a few more hours I thought I had it. I threw the fuse box master switch for one final time – and the electric garage door opened. Clicking the garage light switch to "on" lowered it, but only until the garage light was switched off again.

Was it Achilles or Agamemnon who first licked his wounds? Whoever, he wasn't the last. I locked up and went to bed (it was after midnight).

The next morning was different. I awoke and thought: I've been having nightmares. It was all a dream! Could this be the end of it all?

I was disabused of this by my wife shouting downstairs: "The garage light has been on all night." I got up, went down, and switched it off. The outside security light came on, the utility room light came on, and the garage door opened.

I went indoors and telephoned Barry, the electrician who had wired our house in the first place. "Barry," I said, "I've got a bit of a problem."

Barry isn't cheap, but his work is reliable.

Genre:Non-fiction. Topic: "Astonishment". By Lesley Watts

Winchester Christmas Market

A dreary December day. Not one of those cold bright ones beckoning walks across crisp woodland floors, breath misting, droplets clinging to your clothes. No today it is just dull. Grey skies turning everything into a negative of itself – bleaching colour and making trees look even more menacing and skeletal. Even the Christmas music the radio stations insist on playing from 1st December, does nothing to lift my mood.

A sudden desire to be surrounded by colour leads to a spontaneous decision to visit the Winchester Christmas Market. I reconcile myself to yet more Christmas tunes – unavoidable I fear – but there will be much to distract too ... I hope! The festival of lights begins at the top of the high street, and then disappears from view as the bus takes a circuitous route past the railway station, eventually entering the high street next to King Alfred's statue. He, too, looks quite grey and dreary in the winter's light, but beyond is a kaleidoscope of colour and as I disembark, a wave of noise assaults the senses. And the smells! Christmas spices, hot chocolate, bread... and the butchers' stores – not such a pleasant experience for a vegetarian! How quickly I've gotten out of the habit of 'admiring' the meat stall – my feet move me quickly on!

I leave the High Street market and turn left towards the Cathedral where the huts have been put out for the Christmas market – and am struck by the 'sameness' of the wares. Yes, they're delightful, yes, they're festive, but meandering with the other 'sheep' as though stuck on a conveyor belt on the one-way system, I realise nothing appeals, nothing surprises me. There are the huts selling the same chocolates I bought as a Christmas Day gift for our party of friends last year. There are the tree decorations I gave to my godchildren. There is the festive cider I sampled last year ... well actually that was really nice so maybe I'll buy more! Then I stop in my tracks ... Nestled in behind the ice-skating rink and before the festive hog roast – really! – is a simple stall. Bereft of flashing lights but decorated with simple hand-crafted tree decorations and gifts, together with a message of hope and love from an overseas orphanage being championed by Friends of the Cathedral.

I pause in thought and movement, and realise, to my surprise, that this is the message of Christmas in its simplest form. Strip away the glitz and noise, and reflect on others – perhaps without family, gifts, or even food – to whom Christmas is a different fayre. Humbling ... and I shouldn't be surprised to find this poignant reminder here, but I am.

What started as a day where I was complaining about the weather and being self-centred has now been reset for me;a timely reminder that Christmas is so much more than glitz and noise. Being grateful for what we have without expectation ... family and friends, peace andlove. No surprises there surely?

Genre: Fiction. Topic: "Memories". By Carol Waterkeyn

Darkness and Light

"So, what do you think is troubling you and making it difficult for you to sleep?" My care nurse is asking as she helps me out of bed and into the chair.

"I'm having recurring dreams."

"Well, we'll try giving you a sedative tonight. I'll ask the doctor," she smiles, straightening the bedcovers and leaves so I can wash in the bowl she's brought with her. I think of my re-visiting dream. A nightmare. *She* is a-night-mare. It's like she is telling me something but I don't speak horse language.

She comes to me in my troubled sleep; Jet, the horse that got me through my hours of darkness on the front line at The Somme. Now long gone, killed by machine gun fire, she comes to me in my dreams.

As I stroke her mane, I see her frightened eyes imploring me to take her back to the fields where she once cantered and bucked. I hear her soft whinny. I remember the feel of her once-shiny, almost-black coat after I'd groomed her with the brush. I remember the smell of her leather tack and saddle and the softness of her muzzle. I remember her sweet nature and her bravery; going forward through mud and bullets, and jumping over barbed wire – it's such evil stuff that barbed wire. I had to patch her up several times, but we soldiered on together with our scars, both hidden and outward.

Somehow, I got through the war but, she didn't. We buried her in a field in Picardie after the attack that also left me without a leg. We both lost our comrades. She lost her fellow-horse friends, Star and Hercules, who were interred alongside her, and I lost countless mates.

I actually gave up getting too close to my fellow soldiers. We were what they now call 'cannon fodder', unlikely to survive the next day. But I did survive, thanks to my missing leg, which probably seems a paradox. I went first to the field hospital and then I was shipped back to England to recover without my leg.

I saw out the rest of the war in hospital, then convalescence home, and finally back home on the farm. I had been enlisted in the Bucks Hussars because I could ride a horse, something I was no longer able to do; well certainly not when I was injured. I did relearn after I received my prosthetic leg. My Margaret persuaded me. And, we married when I could manage to walk down the aisle unaided – a proud moment.

Sadly, I lost her two years ago. But I feel proud that we had sixty-five good years of marriage. I miss her every day. The life-changing battle when I lost my horse and my leg was 75 years ago. I'm no longer on the farm that had been in our family for generations. I've been here in Primrose Bank Nursing Home since Margaret passed. I think proudly of our son John who runs the farm now, although he talks of retiring and going to live by the sea. He comes to visit when he can, as do my grandchildren and great grandchildren. I often tell them about Jet, my horse from the war.

After my lunch, I feel tired. I'm going to have a nap. As my eyes close, suddenly I can see Jet, she's coming towards me again in my sleep. This time I climb on her back. I can hardly see as the sun is shining in my face. It's such a bright, white light. For some reason I feel ecstatically happy. I look down, and my missing leg is back somehow. I gently touch Jet's flanks with my two heels and we go off together.

Genre: Fantasy. Topic: "Law". By Tony Wilson

Death in Australasia

Law. Like a phoenix, rising from the ashes of her demise, the girl's back lifted from the raised bed of wood and palm leaves upon which she had been placed. This action seemed to require no effort from her and I gazed in stupefied awe and fear as the Shamanic chants rose to a crescendo above the murmur of the entranced villagers, all intoning the same monotonous note. She swivelled her body, placed her feet on the sand and stood, her long black hair falling around her shoulders. Her naked brown skin glistened with a luminous lustre as it reflected the numerous burning oil lamps encircling her, magnifying the darkness of the night. The shaman shouted out one last piercing chant and her eyes opened. Lifeless eyes as black as her hair stared at me as she raised her arm and like an outstretched arrow pointed her index finger at the centre of my chest.

    I shuddered; my whole naked body covered in beads of sweat. I strained uselessly against the bonds that tightly held me to the bamboo stakes I was lashed to. Her lips parted and from her open mouth seawater seeped down her jaw, her breasts, her thighs and evaporated on the sands. All eyes were on me as the shaman turned also and fixed me with his awful gaze.

    I had always had a wanderlust; as a boy I would skip lessons to go hunting rabbits in the outback. No matter what punishments I was given, I could not be deterred from my lust for adventure. Gaining little education and not caring for the life of a rancher, my disappointed father bid me goodbye at the age of fifteen as his only child travelled to the coast to apprentice as a boatbuilder in Hervey Bay. The harbour was the centre of the Australian whaling industry but we also built fishing boats and fast schooners. I was able, when not working, to crew for fishing vessels working off the waters of the southern tip of the great barrier reef and learned to dive for shellfish. I loved the life, mostly outdoors, I grew tall, tanned and strong but the sea drew me to its deep heart and I yearned to explore it.

    My aim was to cruise the islands of Polynesia for as long as I could. I was to find that a few of the islands I encountered were not on my charts so I added them and gave them names with the intention of informing the Admiralty as I reached any British outposts. Then one day I was sailing casually between a pair of uninhabited atolls, careful of missing any jagged reefs, when I spotted a small dug-out canoe in the water and tacked to approach it. As I closed in on it, I became suddenly aware of bubbles rising to the surface directly before my bow. I could do nothing to avoid hitting the rapidly rising diver as she surfaced. I tacked hard and came around alongside the floating lifeless body, pulled her aboard and tried to revive her. My efforts were fruitless as I rose from my knees, I became aware of figures climbing aboard; they had approached silently on a small flotilla of canoes. They seized me and I was bludgeoned unconscious.

    When I came to, I found myself a captive watching a girl brought back to some kind of zombie life. The shaman approached me, a glint of shining steel in his hand. His words were meaningless to me, yet, as he plunged the knife deep into my chest, as life drained from me and I floated between this life and the next his words crystallised in my mind and I understood them. He said, "A life for a life, this is our law".

Genre: Fiction. Topic: "Law". By Helen Griffith

Minor catastrophe

Minnie and Morris had just bought a campervan. Minnie envisaged their retirement being full of trips to the far-flung corners of the UK and Europe. No ties, just peaceful living, communing with nature; up with the lark; full of the joie de vivre. Of course, what Minnie wanted she usually got. Morris was quite aware that the success of forty-three years of marriage was to nod in all the right places and tread carefully when answering a question. Morris was more of a wake-up-in-a-comfortable-bed-followed-by-a-full-English-breakfast guy but when Minnie had a bee in her bonnet, then he wouldn't hear the last of it. Besides, campervans held their value, didn't they? He decided to buy into her dream and sell when reality kicked in.

The campervan they acquired was best described much like themselves – seen better days but life in the old gal yet! A full set of matching accessories were duly bought from IKEA. Then came the task of deciding where to go. Coincidentally, a new series called *Britain on Film* on BBC1 visited various places that had been captured in films and television series. Inspired by this, Minnie decided that they should go to Port Isaac in Cornwall, so she could tread in the steps of her beloved *Doc Martin*.

And so, the day arrived. They set off on a bright and sunny morning. However, as there was no air conditioning, by the time they joined the traffic jam at Portishead they were hot and irritable. This was further compounded by missing a planned lunch in a

Dartmoor pub. Hungry and tired, hot and bothered, Minnie was wondering if they would ever get to their destination.

Sergeant Colin Tubbs was the community policeman and had been serving Port Isaac and district for many years. In turn, the good people served him well with local fayre. Tubbs by name and Tubbs by nature, he was only happy to consume everything that came his way; from sausage rolls and pasties to freshly baked scones with lashings of jam and clotted cream (in that sequence of course!). Recently though, Mrs Tubbs had been nagging him to lose a few inches around the waist. Reluctantly, he enrolled at the local gym and was now rather proud of the muscles he was developing.

Tubbs was tootling along the coast road when he came to a bend and noticed that the wooden crash fencing was missing. He stopped the car and went to investigate. Peering down, he saw a campervan wedged between two trees about ten feet below him.

"Oh lummy," he thought and immediately called it in.

"Are you okay?" He shouted down the slope.

"Yes," came a shaky response.

"Okay, don't move!" he called over his shoulder as he ran back to his car to get some rope.

Shimming down the slope, hanging on to the trees and shrubbery around, he quickly tied it to the axle and then secured it around a nearby tree. Looking at his efforts, he felt that the campervan was not particularly secure and that he couldn't afford to wait for the emergency services.

In the cabin, Morris and Minnie were bruised and battered and gazing down on the bright blue sea below them. Minnie had just started whimpering when her passenger door opened and there appeared a red-faced policeman hanging onto a tree branch and extending his hand towards her.

"Quick! Gently undo your seat belt and come to me. Try not to make any sudden movements." Tubbs' voice was calm and assertive.

Minnie grabbed his hand and allowed herself to be manhandled up the slope to the road.

The van groaned and inched forward. Realising that there was little time left, Tubbs went back for Morris. Just as Morris jumped, the van shifted again and for a moment Tubbs' grasp was all that was stopping Morris from slipping down the steep slope. Drawing all his resources together, Tubbs managed to pull him up and together they made it to the road just as the emergency services were arriving on full blues and twos. Before they had time to thank him, Minnie and Morris were whipped off to hospital for a full check-up.

A disaster was averted!

The next day the local paper carried the following headline:

"Dramatic rescue by the strong arm of the law."

"An amazing rescue took place yesterday on the cliff road just outside Port Isaac. Sergeant Tubbs showed selfless bravery as he single-handedly pulled two stranded tourists from their campervan.

Mr and Mrs Minor said they have no idea what happened. One moment they were on the road; next minute they were headed down the cliff. 'We owe our lives to Sergeant Tubbs'they said. 'He showed tremendous bravery and we don't know what would have happened if he had not acted so decisively. We were visiting places that have been on television. We've now decided that these places are better viewed through a screen! Our campervan days are over!'"

Genre: Fiction. Topic: "Danger". By Viv Gough

NI Danger

Northern Ireland in 1973 and the Murphy household is in its usual Monday morning chaos.

"Cieran, have you got your lunch box?" "Sarah, where is your other shoe?" "Oh God, where are the car keys?"

The dog is barking. Sarah kicks its bowl looking for her shoe.

"Patrick, have you seen my car keys?"

"No, sorry, and I haven't time to look, I'm late. Got to go, bye-eee!"

Cheryl throws up her hands in frustration.

"You think I'm not late too? But, never mind. You go. Don't worry about me, I'll cope, I always do."

She scowls at his back and the door shuts behind her husband.

The key search continues until they are found under the tea towel.Then the doorbell rings.

"Blast! What now?"

By the time Cheryl opens the door. The bell pusher has gone but there is a brown, paper-wrapped, square parcel on the doorstep. It is addressed to P Murphy. Cheryl assumes that it's the new part for Patrick's bike that he's been waiting for. They said a courier would deliver it. She would normally open it for him but, this morning, she doesn't have time. In her rush to get going, she plonks it on the hall table and the family leave the house. The dog whines, puts its tail between its legs and lies down behind the closed front door. The house is silent – apart from a gentle tick, tick, tick – from the parcel.

10.00am. The Murphy's cleaner arrives. She shoos the dog out of the way, throws her coat over the banister and switches on the tape deck. She puts in Status Quo and puts the kettle on. With a sigh she surveys the kitchen and wonders where to start. She manoeuvres the vacuum round the floor in jerky circles to the beat of 'Caroline' and the parcel gets moved to the dog's basket to facilitate the dusting of the hall table. She leaves. The dog hides under the table, deprived of his comfy bed and there is silence once more, apart from the ticking.

12.00pm. The dog walker arrives to be welcomed with excited barking and lots of face-licking. The out-of-work young actor is glad of the few pounds he can earn whilst jogging with the dog through the park. He puts in his ear piece and adjusts his mini radio, attaches the dog-lead to the dog's collar and off they run, leaving the parcel to tick alone.

1.00pm. Back home and the knackered dog has a noisy slurp from his bowl. The young man refills it, moves the parcel from dog bed to draining board, ruffles the dog's head and leaves for his next doggy appointment. The dog is asleep within seconds. The parcel isn't.

3.45pm. The sound of a key in the lock causes the dog to bark again and there is more face-licking as the children arrive home from school with Grandma. Laughter and moaning pervade the kitchen as kindly authority orders hands to be washed. A picnic in the garden is decided on and Grandma butters bread and produces her homemade Irish tea cake. She lays a cloth on the lawn and instructs Cieran to find something sturdy to stand the tray of drinks on. He chooses the parcel on the draining board, covers it with the tea towel and takes it outside. The birds chirp, the water feature in the pond creates a soothing gurgling sound, the bees and Grandma hum and the ticking goes on unnoticed.

6.00pm. Patrick and Cheryl arrive home at the same time.

"Hi Mummy," says Sarah. "We had a picnic."

Grandma smiles.

"The rain brought us in but the dog is still running around getting muddy outside."

Police Sergeant Patrick Murphy takes off his civilian jacket to reveal his RUC uniform. He looks out of the window.

"What's the dog playing with? It looks like soggy brown paper."

"Oh crikey! Sorry Dad," says Cieran. "I used the parcel to stand the drinks on. I forgot it was still out there."

"What parcel?"

"I think your bike part arrived this morning but I didn't have time to open it," said Cheryl.

"That arrived on Saturday," says Patrick. He takes a sharp intake of breath.

"Oh, my God! What have I told you about taking in parcels when I'm not here?"

He screams as he charges outside. "Get away from the window!"

The dog flees as Patrick runs down the garden and grabs the parcel. He throws it towards the pond as he flattens himself onto the lawn.

At 6.30pm precisely, an explosion scatters goldfish to four corners of the garden.

6.31pm. The day for the parcel has ended, and it ticks no more.

Genre:Fiction.Topic:"Astonishment".By Jan Mills

Divorce

Sally was certain Mark was having an affair – it was obvious when you looked at the clues and put them all together. She grabbed her iPad and opened the questionnaire she had been browsing:

Do you suspect your partner of infidelity?

Has his behaviour changed in recent months? – check

Has he lost weight or seems to be trying to get more fit? – check

Is he taking more care of his appearance? – check

Is he going out alone more than before? – check.

In the last three months Mark had been meeting a "work colleague" for a game of badminton twice a week. So why did he wear nice clothes and, especially, his best shoes? Who was this work colleague and what exercise did they really do?

Mark worked for an advertising agency and was surrounded at work by attractive and mostly unattached young women. Although upset with him, Sally had to admit that after almost 25 years of marriage he had aged little and was still a good-looking man. He had lost some weight recently and was looking fit and toned. She looked at herself in the mirror; her eyes had bags beneath them and she had put on a bit of weight over the past five years. Her hair was okay, if helped a bit by a bottle, but she was beginning to look her age. Should Sally challenge Mark? She might lose him and they had too much to let it go without a fight: three loving, adult children, a comfortable home and lifestyle and, she had thought, a happy marriage.

Sally made a decision – she would fight hard and dirty if necessary.

Over the next two months she put all her effort into self-improvement. She joined a gym, found a personal trainer, lost weight and had some regular beauty treatments. She was now looking great and with a new wardrobe, thanks to her "Colour Consultant", she was looking at least ten years younger.

Mark was certain Sally was having an affair – it was obvious when you looked at the clues and put them all together. Sally had changed dramatically over the past two months and was now looking much as she had when he first fell in love with her. What was he to do? He had thought they had a good marriage and he didn't want to lose her. It was their Silver Wedding Anniversary in a few weeks and he had planned what he had hoped would be a wonderful surprise for her.

Sally was feeling quite desperate by now and she and Mark were avoiding any serious conversation with each other. She made a provisional appointment to meet with a Solicitor, just to get an idea of procedure if they did decide to divorce. Her heart was heavy as she contemplated their "celebration" in a week's time. Their children and partners were taking them out for a meal to celebrate their anniversary.

Mark had put in so much time and effort to be ready for their anniversary party and now he did not even know if Sally wanted to be with him anymore. She thought they were going to have a meal with the kids, but he had planned an altogether different evening for Sally. They would be having a party with family and friends and he had even hired a live band. Sally had always loved dancing, although he usually avoided it as he had three left feet.

On the night of the party Sally looked stunning. She had put everything into getting ready; if this was to be their last "big date" together, it would be memorable. As they entered the banquet room at the hotel, Sally was satisfyingly surprised to see so many of their family and friends there. When the band started to play Mark took Sally's hand and led her to the dance floor. She was bemused – Mark did not dance, but she was about to find out his secret. His steps were perfect as he twirled her in a waltz and a foxtrot and skipped across the floor in a quickstep.

Suddenly Sally realised what Mark had been doing for the last few months. She was astonished!

Genre: Fiction. Topic: "Danger". By Ted Mason

Armageddon

Following a long and controversial Cobra meeting on an Island in the Aegean, Major General Collins instructed Colonel I/C Northern Hemisphere to proceed with Operation First Strike from the hidden,ultra-secret base that was in complete control of missile silos placed all over Europe.

All available data on the mission was uploaded into the artificial intelligence software of the strike plane, including target references to the nuclear missile attached to its under-belly. Barbara slowly manoeuvred to runway 4, aware that this mission would create the largest nuclear airburst ever used against the Russian Federation. It would be a suicide mission.

Final checks complete, she accelerated to take off speed and climbed to 10,000 feet. New and top-secret developments in power and speed shot the craft forward, and enabling it to stay in the air for longer than any other plane. Barbara once again checked fuel consumption, and bearings. She chose the safest approach to Vyatskye, North East of the Russian city of Kasan on the Volga River. All data suggested it would be a flight time of 3.4 hours from the secret air base on the Turkish island of Chios, East between the mountains of Sivasli, then North over the Black Sea at wave height, and North East over the Sea of Azov. After that it would be a hazardous flight up the Volga at night, hugging the water to avoid radar. There were other alternatives but this was the best chance of mission success.

Barbara shut down unnecessary equipment and data flow in order to maximise the rate of response to navigation data. There was little more she could do now until she had to leave the river at Dimitrovgrad, to avoid detection at the City of Kazan, and then fly North East to the huge nuclear missile control facility at Vyatskye that was her target.

The AI navigation A was preset so Barbara settled down to think for a couple of hours. To utilise the time, she thought over the data for the last time. The probability of Russia launching nuclear strikes at NATO forces and cities within 10 days was at 72 percent. The probability of mission success was 87 percent. The probability of retaliatory strikes was high but Cobra determined collateral death and damage to be acceptable. How many deaths are acceptable? Barbara called up information on nuclear airbursts, radiation clouds, wind speed and direction. She analysed population densities and medical information and wondered at how a few individuals could consider such atrocities. She had not considered the cost of her mission before.

"Confirm mission objectives," she signalled at millisecond speed to avoid radio detection. "Mission confirmed."

I wonder what it is like to die? Or is it the manner of death that people fear? Barbara was too young to have thought about any of this. Now the thought of dying in a suicide mission frightened her. Were there better alternatives for the mission that involved less harm? She downloaded tactical strike data to see if there was a better way of avoiding a nuclear catastrophe. Only one stood out. It was not ideal. People would still die but it was a matter of numbers, and Barbara was good at numbers. Her plan would harm fewer people.

Barbara fed in new navigational vectors and watched the controls veer the plane around 180 degrees. Before she de-activated the communication systems, she recorded a delayed message to Cobra Base and to Russian communication detectors. She anticipated their reactions and re-examined the data as she sped home. Maybe she would not die today.

She began to question what it all meant. Who should decide who would live and who would die? What was the point of life anyway? Why should she be ordered to die in a mission that would destroy so much? How is it that she had been given so much power; the power to help mankind or kill it?

Well, Barbara's decision was clear and reasoned, considering the vast information available to her. She had been given the ability to make decisions for herself and she was determined to do the right thing. She flew almost at wave height across the Black Sea and over the coast of Turkey. Undetected, the plane weaved through narrow valleys over Ismir towards Chios. Her plane had succeeded in flying right over Russia undetected, and now she was avoiding NATO radar installations as she flew over the Aegean.

...

Confusion in Mission Control on Chios was giving way to panic. No nuclear detonation had been detected anywhere in the Northern hemisphere. Should they stand down all the missile silos throughout Europe or continue with the first strike plans? If the mission had failed, the Eastern bloc would have the advantage!

Satellite observations showed several small planes on various flight paths across the Aegean but only one had no transponder signal. Why was Barbara returning to base? Had there been a fault with the nuclear device? If so, she would surely have adjusted her strategy. Yes, thousands of people would die in the blast but global war would be postponed, if not averted.

...

60 seconds before dropping her payload, Barbara wondered what it would be like to die in the blast. She quickly brought up data about religious views on death, the afterlife and Gods. Her signals were sent 20 seconds before the bomb dropped; one translated into Russian. "I am death. I am God. I decide who is to live and who is to die".

For a split second, Barbara felt her brain circuits fry as she was blown out of existence.

Genre: Fiction. Topic: "Law". By Lesley Watts

Just Law

I'm Luke Alexander Wilson although at Uni. I'm also known as "just Law". "Just Law" has me smiling as I've tried to follow the rules but it hasn't always been easy. Let me explain: my parents split up when I was 15 and my dad disappeared without a forwarding address or any financial support for me, my mum or my two younger siblings. So overnight I didn't become the "man of the house", but I had to step up, supporting mum and at times being an unpaid babysitter. Mum worked shifts cleaning offices and stacking shelves at Tesco and when she was working, I was given responsibility for looking after Jake, 7 and Chloe, 9, which seriously curtailed my after school social-life, although looking back at times was no bad thing.

Despite some peer pressure and promises of extra money – which I must admit would have been useful and tempting – I stayed away from the local gangs, their drug dealings, running messages and such, shielding my siblings as well as myself. Mum desperately wanted us to have futures and opportunities and always drummed into us the importance of school so in between sibling duties, I studied towards my GCSEs, then 'A' levels … getting good enough grades to study Sports Science at University.

Oh yes, did I mention I'm a pretty fast runner, which comes in handy for weekend rugby – andalso as it happens escaping from celebratory shenanigans that at times can get out of hand! My best mate at Uni is Aaron and he's getting a reputation for being overzealous, flirtatious and unable to hold his tongue or cheap beer at our post-match pub crawls. When his mouth runs off with the local lads and handbags are drawn it really is best to make ourselves scarce as quickly as possible. More running practice! One such weekend saw our usual artful dodger skills coming dramatically undone.

The local lads took umbrage at Aaron flirting with their girls; there was some pushing and shoving, glasses were broken when I fell into a table, and mayhem ensued. Unfortunately, the local lads happened to be more sober than our party … and off-duty policemen! Who knew? The old adage about police getting younger was so true … until their more senior colleagues waded in and "felt our collars".

Now for team selection and not to mention careers moving forward, it's important that I keep my nose and record clean – not to mention avoiding disappointing mum! So, a night in cells whilst Aaron and others sobered up sufficiently to receive warnings and a shared bill for damages, gave pause for thought. On this occasion I really was in the wrong place at the wrong time as I was the nominated sober one chaperoning but events got out of hand. Guilty by association did feel unfair but no arguments about my party's culpability. The whole experience was worrying but also enlightening. Seeing a police station and all its moving parts working like a well-oiled machine on a Saturday night, gave me renewed respect for the police. The camaraderie of the officers and the support they gave to the public for a myriad of events had me enthralled … and thinking.

Being sober I soaked up the experience and chatted to the police on duty when I could throughout the night, and by morning had decided to look more into the role of being a special constable – with its added bonus of looking good on my CV, gaining extra-curricular points and maybe even a step towards a future career in the police, or some other way using law to help others … and if I could combine that with my fitness and sports interests, say playing for a police rugby team, all the better. It also spoke to my nurturing side – I thought back to my siblings and my more recent role of looking out for my Uni mates. It's early days, but who knows "just Law" may have a more literal meaning in the future!

Genre: Fiction. Topic: "Surprise". By Alan Pearce

Eustace

Verwood

14th May 2023

The Managing Director
The Small White Delivery Van Company
Bournemouth

Dear Sir or Madam

I write to introduce myself as Pastor Philip Perkins of the Verwood Evangelical Temperance Redemption

Church. Please do not stop reading; I am not trying to preach – this letter is about a very practical matter which I think you may be able to help out with, and might be to your benefit.

Until last week I used to give talks in village halls etc. about the evils of alcohol, and in order to get (and keep) people's attention I used to have an incapable, unreformable alcoholic idiot called Eustace sitting on the stage edge, legs dangling, dribbling and drooling, mumbling and coughing from both ends, until he fell off. He was completely helpless, and totally useless, but we looked after him well and made sure he was as comfortable as could be. Sadly, he passed away over the weekend.

Just this morning, at 11.35, one of your vehicles Registration Number HG22 PFV, pulled out of Black Moor Road into the B3081 traffic without looking or caring, causing me to swerve and hit the kerb and a vehicle coming the other way to mount the pavement. The driver then sped off at about 60 mph, weaving through the Verwood town centre traffic.

I wonder if I might borrow this idiot for a while, to replace Eustace until I can find a permanent replacement?

Yours faithfully

Alan Pearce
(p.p.) dictated by the Pastor

Genre: Non-fiction. Topic: "People". By Ted Mason

The race

Sam Peevis hated the PE teacher. There he was with no PE shorts because they had ripped when he had pulled them over his head earlier. Sam was shaking. He was standing in the changing room in a dirty T shirt. He was thinking about Mr Moyse who was about to appear like a thunder storm.

"Lend me some shorts, Tony," he begged.

"Get some from the lost property bag. You're not having mine."

Sam held his nose as he fumbled around in a large plastic bag of stinking abandoned kit. Finally, he found a small pair of shorts and was easing his big bottom into them as the changing room door opened.

"Well, it is nice to have you in some kit, Peevis," Moyse grinned. "Right lads, join the girls for a little run."

Sam was the first to run out, not because he wanted to be away from Mr Moyse. He hit the cold air and shivered. The teacher was holding clip-boards and pencils.

"Today we are timing you. You're going through the woods and down to the bottom field, then follow the lane back to the school woods and our field."

All the children were moving to the start. Some looked enthusiastic and some, like Sam, showed how miserable they were. He decided to walk fast instead of running. In that way he might just get to finish without dying.

"Ready... Go!" Mr Moyse yelled near Sam's ear.

"Get out the way, Peevis," Tony shouted as he slowed down and bumped into him. Sam fell back as the main group of runners passed and headed for the trees.

Sam's bedroom looked out over these trees and he often stood at his window looking at them. He reached the cover of the first bushes. At least Moyse could not see him now. He was safe to stop and rest, and walk slowly.

Sam was now all alone. He pulled his shorts down a little to stop them cutting into his bottom. He could see his house now, just over an old wooden fence at the edge of the woods. And there was the gap in the fence.

He stepped through the gap and headed for the back door. The house was empty. He could just have a quick drink and return to the woods before anyone noticed. He would stay here until he saw the first of the runners pass on their final circuit. He could then join the race and finish without anyone knowing.

He smiled as he sipped a hot cup of tea. Panic struck Sam as he saw Mark appearing for the last time. He ran for the back door and hurried to the gap in the fence. He could see Tony and Sally just coming around the oak tree. He waited until they had passed and ran behind them. They were then out of the wood and onto the playing field. The finish was just fifty metres away. Mr Moyse was shouting encouragement to the leaders; Douglas, Mark, Tony and Sally and ... Mr Moyse suddenly went quiet and stood with his mouth open. Peevis! "Come on boy, run," he began shouting again. For the first time ever, Sam smiled at his teacher's words.

"Good boy, Sam. You've beaten Frankie Smith! Mark, Douglas, Tony, Sally, Sam and Frankie... over here, and you Peevis," called the teacher, "Well done. You will represent the school in the County School's Cross-Country competition tomorrow. I'll have a letter for you to take home tonight.

Sam suddenly looked rather unwell! Later that day, his science teacher had never had such a good lesson because Sam was so well behaved. There were no rude noises and no silly answers from the worst pupil in the school! All Sam could think about was running and coming last, with hundreds of children from all the schools in the county watching. He even mumbled a "thankyou" to Mr Moyse when handed a letter to take home.

"You are late home again. More trouble at school I suppose. Why can't you keep out of trouble?" Sam's mother moaned. "Let me see your school bag. I suppose you have another letter about behaviour. Where is it?"

She held out her hand, palm upwards. Sam rummaged in his bag. As he took it out of a side pocket his mother was not angry. It was worse, because she sighed. There were tears in her eyes. "I knew it."

She slowly took the envelope without opening it, and placed it on the kitchen table.

"But it's ...," began Sam.

"Go to your room Sam," so Sam pushed past her to the stairs without finishing the "good" news. After a long twenty minutes, Sam decided to tell his mum everything. She was not in the kitchen. Nor was she in the back yard or her room, and Sam noticed that the letter was not on the table. Then the back door opened and his mother bounced into the kitchen smiling. She held out a plastic bag.

"I have got us your favourite. Hamburger, chips, chocolate cake and a bottle of coke. Why didn't you tell me? You bad boy." She grabbed Sam in a huge hug. "My Sam in a big running competition. Who'd have thought?"

That evening was the happiest they had enjoyed for a long time, until Sam lay in bed and began to come back to reality. What would happen tomorrow? He had not told his mother about the ripped shorts. What would he wear? The next morning his mum had mended his shorts and washed his T shirt, too. She grinned as she told him that she would take time off work to come to see him run.

After lunch, Sam got changed early. He wandered out onto the field and looked at Mr Moyse laughing very loudly with a very fat lady wearing an enormous track-suit. Then he saw his mother.

"There you are dear. I got an hour off work to come to see you. I'll be just over there, love." She pointed to the edge of the field and left Sam to quiver with fear. Was it too late to tell Mr Moyse the truth? He was only a few metres away. He and his mother would be angry but that would be better than being laughed at by everyone when he came last. Sam edged towards Mr Moyse, who peered down at him, looking worried.

"Please Sir, about the run yesterday. I didn't..." he began. But he was interrupted.

"Ah Samuel. Wanted to speak with you. You must be excited. Unfortunately, we are only allowed four competitors and not six, and as you were fifth, you will not be able to run. I am so sorry. You must be very disappointed. I will tell your mum. Is she here?"

"Er... um. She's over there," Sam muttered, pointing to the crowd.

As Mr Moyse strolled towards the crowd, Sam finally burst with emotion. Tears ran down his nose as he sank to the grass in a happy daze. What luck! He was saved. The nightmare was over.

"Oh Sam. Mr Moyse told me. I'm still very proud of you," said his mum softly. She dabbed his eyes with her handkerchief. "He says you can run in the next competition if you want. Now get changed and we can go to the cinema later."

Sam walked to the changing room. He plonked himself onto a bench and looked at all the children's clothes spread over the hooks. There were Tony's trousers. Oh dear! Sam laughed wickedly. He took the trousers and looked towards the toilets. He smiled as he walked to the first cubicle and flushed them down the toilet. They were too big to disappear but looked wonderful wedged in the U-bend.

Genre: Non-fiction. Topic: "Astonishment". By Tony Wilson

Canyon

We started out on highway sixty-four from Williams. Leaving the town behind after a quick breakfast and also leaving the steady flow of traffic on route forty, we ventured north on the much quieter uphill road into the desert. Fifty-nine miles of relentless and gradually rising tarmac straight as an arrow. The Sun had risen in the still, cloudless Arizona sky and with it the mercury, heralding another mercilessly hot day, yet as we drove on, the increasing altitude kept pace with the temperature causing it to plateau in the mid-thirties centigrade. At least for the morning.

The hills gradually fell behind us, leaving a featureless terrain, except for the numerous cacti eking an existence out of the arid soil. We passed one township on the journey, where the road was joined by highway one-eighty. With the last petrol station receding in the rear window we continued on the dusty desert road, keeping to Rule fifty-five, that is the fifty-five miles per hour speed limit existing at that time throughout the whole United States of America, to save fuel.

At long last the road bisected right and left. We took the westbound arm and found ourselves bordered on the right by a hedge of shortish fir trees. We both thought we must be very close by now, so I pulled the car over and parked by the roadside. We alighted and were shocked by the heated air as it filled our lungs, after the comfort of our air-conditioned Chevrolet Impala, combined with the altitude of six-thousand feet, it made our progress a little sluggish. Walking through the small gaps in the fir trees, nothing prepared us for the astonishing scene that opened before us at Yavapai Point. It is difficult to explain the overwhelming assault on our senses, the spectacle and natural majesty of one of the world's greatest wonders that is the Grand Canyon.

At this point of the canyon the opposing rim is ten miles away, yet the trees were so clear above the impossibly beautiful rock formations. The mind is given so much visual information that is almost impossible to process. I remember my jaw literally dropping! Of course, we had both seen photographs and movies in the past but, it simply did not relate to what was around us.

The canyon walls are a hundred shades of colour as they fall in sheer drops, ledges and cascades of rock, gradually closing in towards one another until they meet the Colorado river meandering like an azure snake a mile below us. Six-million years of successive waves of glacial action have carved this amazing feature onto the surface of Arizona, scarring it so deeply that waters from an entire sea would barely fill the abyss;this chasm of multiple facets and multitude of rock formations.

We could see only a fraction of the canyon from our vantage point yet it more than filled our vision as it expanded beyond our horizons, physically and metaphysically.

So much sky and rock and heat and shock!

Genre: Fiction. Topic: "Fear". By Alan Pearce

A dark story

Duncan was the investment director of a huge multinational bonds company, with a salary in excess of six figures and a leverage finger in nearly every financial institution in the world. He was indeed a fortunate man. He could afford almost anything he wanted to make his personal lifestyle pleasant. He had a fleet of cars for every occasion; city, country and overseas residences; and a host of adoring acolytes whom he kept well paid. He was, to put it mildly, more than comfortable.

Each day he would rise at seven, wash, shave, dress and go down for breakfast, which the cook and maid had laid out and served for him. His wife would come down later, after he had gone to the office. He saw her briefly in the evening. At first, they used to talk over dinner, but in later years they had both lapsed into silence. Duncan was hardly surprised when he learned that his wife was leading a quite different private life while he was at work. She was cheating on him in a big way, with a wide variety of lovers.

Sadly, he allowed this situation to continue – he wanted no ripples in his money-acquiring career. But social intercourse waned and, in the end, each was living their own private life, just snapping at each other from time to time. Not shouting, no violence. It was a sort of living, homeostatic compromise.

Then one day there was a drastic change to his routine. It came in the form of a scruffy envelope in the post, to their home, unstamped. Duncan put it in his pocket and opened it only in the privacy of his office. Various bits of newspaper stuck to a sheet said "Unless you pay us a large sum of money, you will suffer. We will be in touch to tell you how much. Do not go to the police."

Duncan thought deeply about why he should be the victim of this. All his financial dealings, whilst being tough and competitive, were above board. He began to wonder what they had on him and then concluded that whatever it was it wasn't worth "a large sum of money". Probably a hoax, anyway. He didn't go to the police. In fact, he just ignored it.

It wasn't what he thought at all. Nothing to do with his financial dealings. But he was about to find out. When he arrived home three days after this, he was met by the weeping housekeeper who cringed and told him that his wife: "had gone off in a big car with two men, who had left a note". It was on the hall table. He took it to his study and opened it. It just said: "We have got your wife. We are going to dispose of her in a very nasty way unless you deposit five million pounds into a Swiss bank account, details of which we will give you when you telephone the number below – it is a momentary telephone number lasting for 30 seconds only, prepaid for 24 hours only, and will expire at 6pm today. Be sure to 'phone by then".

Duncan was electrified, shocked into action. He had to do something about his wife, and quickly. No time to waste. It was half past five so he had just half an hour to resolve the situation. He made his mind up very quickly.

He telephoned the number. He heard an electronically scrambled voice.

"Who... who are you?" asked Duncan tremulously.

"You don't need to know that," was the reply, "Just that we've got your wife and we will do what we said unless you pay up. We *must* now do what we said to maintain our credibility – we don't want to lose customers, do we? They've got to believe us, or they wouldn't pay. So, you have exactly 48 hours. Put the five million into this untraceable account the number of which I will now give you. Are you ready?"

There was a pause.

Then: "Don't bother," said Duncan. "I won't be paying."

Genre: Poetry. A Few Limericks. By various

There was a young lady from Dorset
Who thought she was in with the horse set
She rode a fine bay
Which bolted one day
So she lived to regret her fine horse pet.

A fellow from Bournemouth, no, Poole
Said:"I may be a bit of a fool
But I know it's not Dorset
And that is becorset
'S like Christchurch – it's got its Home Rule".

There was an old miser called Ray
Who decided to join u3a
When asked for subscription
He had a conniption
Passed out, and just faded away.

A woman who visited Slough
Contracted a terrible cough
She said "it's quite tough"
But suffered on through.
I 'm sure she'll get over it, though.

Now, Tony loved everything old
That shone in the stories he told
His passion for history
Showed many a mystery
And allowed secret tales to unfold.

Barbara's villains and crime,
Convicts serving their time.
Although such a lady
Her tales were quite shady
But her endings were always sublime.

Alan took his new role very seriously
Some felt it was rather imperiously
His group's talents were rare
And they wrote with such flair
That he read all their work quite deliriously.

A fellow from Milford on Sea,
Whose limericks end at line three,
Astounded us all.

Another who came from there, too,
Wrote verses that end at line two

A woman from near Mannington…

Genre: Fiction. Topic: "Surprise". By Viv Gough

Goodbye to George

As I arrive at gate 9 to wait for my flight, I find a quiet spot and take the tin out of my backpack to contemplate my life with George.

"Look at you! A tin of Christmas shortbread comes to mind. The undertakers call it an 'urn' but that makes me think of the WI and tea. Did you see my mother's crocodile tears at your cremation? Sorry! Stupid question. Of course you didn't. She never did approve of you. She said you were all talk and no action and I could do better for myself. She was correct to a point but I loved you anyway. I can't use you to get away from her now. When I visited her, I used to tell her I had to get home to cook your dinner as you were on the late shift. You never were but it sounded feasible. She said I should put a shelf up in our bedroom and put you on it so that you can keep an eye on me. I don't think so!"

The smart young lady at the boarding desk informs us that our flight will be boarding in fifteen minutes and a fellow passenger looks away as I continue my one-way conversation.

"Tom has suggested that I could use you to fertilise your beloved roses. He said you were always full of manure and would approve of organic with no pesticides added. You know your son, always speaks his mind. Trouble is, the cats use the rose bed as a toilet and you're not here to throw buckets of water at them like you used to.

"When I met you, George, you fancied yourself as a free spirit. You were full of ideas for great adventures but in reality, you never had any. I blamed myself for a long time because we had the children early and got bogged down with nappies, schooling, a mortgage and debt and I felt that you were being held back but, with hindsight, I don't think that was really the case. I think we were your comfort zone and the excuse not to take risks. Your high blood pressure was the result of promotion and more responsibility.

"Don't worry that I will scatter you at sea. I know how much you hated water. Do you remember Dawlish when Tom was six? Out on that pedalo, all you did was moan. 'Don't go too fast, stop leaning out, don't go out of our depth!' You were wetting your trunks. Good job it didn't show, they were wet anyway. It was me that taught Tom and Angela to swim because you didn't want to be seen in armbands. For an intelligent man, you had some funny ideas. You always said that if I went first, you would scatter me in the shopping precinct – preferably outside Clark's shoe shop."

The tannoy once again interrupts my conversation with George. "Your flight to Geneva is ready to board. Will rows numbered 1-15 have their passes ready please."

"That's us, George. Time to go. You always said that you wanted to be scattered on Mont Blanc as the air was cleaner, it would be peaceful and nearer to Heaven. You got the idea from your National Geographic magazines. I had laughed and told you I would book some skiing lessons. How on earth did you think I could arrange that? 'Easy,' you said. 'Just take a flight over the Alps and drop me out.'

"Yeah, sure! Open the window and we'll all go with you." You said not to be so stupid and put me down the loo and when I flushed, you would float down on the wind and be where you wanted to be. Well, it doesn't work like that, dear. The toilet tank is emptied on arrival at the destination and probably tipped into the sewers. I know I called you a rat sometimes but I wouldn't want you ending up with them. When I get home and the kids ask me what I eventually did with you, I will tell them that I took you on your first and last adventure. I did take those skiing lessons and I am taking you to Mont Blanc. Do you remember when we first met? You said that I blew you away. In a couple of days, I will do it all over again."

I put George back in my bag and climb the steps and I whisper very quietly to myself, "I will always love you. Are you ready George? Your adventure starts now."

Genre: Fact-based story. Topic:Understanding". By Alan Pearce

Misunderstanding

I visited South Korea in May 1968 as part of a diplomatic mission to promote understanding. At that time the word "understanding" was very significant. The Far East was still in turmoil after the Second

World War and the Korean War and, it was important that nations and organisations who did not trust each other should at least try to understand each other. There was a slight possibility that homeostatic peace might prevail.

My own little sojourn into understanding – or misunderstanding – was actually of little consequence but of wry amusement, perhaps.

We all stayed in a very large hotel. Quite comfortable. It was a two-day event.

On the first morning I came down to breakfast in my naval uniform and met a Korean chap in similar uniform at the buffet counter. I looked at him, held my hand out and said: "Alan Pearce." He bowed, shook my hand and said: "Jo-ann Akhim-Injo." We smiled, but we neither had each other's language.

Jo-ann seemed to be quite a good chap, and we had breakfast in pleasantry and peace – and a complete lack of verbal understanding, but achieving a lot using sign language. The conference itself was simultaneously interpreted, so no problem there.

The first day of the conference achieved nothing. But at least lines of communication were still open. We might be able to achieve something on the morrow.

That evening the British Embassy Korean interpreter engaged me in conversation in the bar.

"Met anybody interesting?" he said.

"Yes," I replied, "fellow called Jo-ann. Funny name for a bloke. Second name's Akhim-Injo. He's military, like me."

He smiled indulgently and said in a somewhat superior tone:"Actually, 'ja ann akhim injo' in Korean means 'Good Morning'."

"Oh," I thought. "Bloody Hell." But still time to recover the situation.

So next morning, I made sure I was down to breakfast first. I met him again at the buffet counter, held out my hand and said: "Ja annakhiminjo."

He shook my hand warmly, bowed and said: "Alan Pearce."

Genre: Fantasy. Topic:"Fashion". By Ted Mason

Trousers

In my wardrobe, tucked right at the back, lie my crumpled, old, flared trousers. They lie curled up in a cold, dark corner as if frightened to be found. If they were a child, he or she would be a starved skeletal urchin, neglected and abused.

Once they were confident and proud, specially made from the finest of fabrics, cut and sewed to perfection. The legs were flared out at the bottom to a width of eight inches. Pointed, black, suede shoes would peep from beneath the hems, yet the waist was small and they were tight around the hips. They had a shiny zip instead of ugly fly buttons, but best of all was a wide, bright yellow belt. When worn, they were pulled right up tight to show off every bump and curve. Ah, what nights those trousers remembered; strutting and dancing in nightclubs and discos, attracting attention from skinny girls in Mary Quant miniskirts and trouser suits.

At first, they were worn only in the evenings for special times such as meeting friends or sometimes a girlfriend if I was lucky. At the clubs there was no competition with my trousers... except maybe that hippy in a see-through lace shirt! Maybe if the trousers could get together with the lace shirt... oh what joy that would be!

And then came the day when two changes were made. The first was the thrill of them being worn out in the daytime. Those day trips into the city were wonderful. Strolling down crowded streets with young girls turning their heads in admiration, and old biddies tut-tutting about "young people today". I would spend hours in fashionable boutiques and my trousers would unkindly criticise those on the rails that were unsold. Friends would meet in coffee houses where they would admire the silks and satins. These were happy times. But another change was in the bedroom.

At the end of the day my trousers would just be thrown unfolded and un-hung, on the bed. Newer trousers began taking their place and no longer were they chosen for evening adventures. Flares were becoming unfashionable, and skin tight legs all the way to the bottom were the rage. No belt but red braces, a white shirt sporting a black string tie, a long tailed, dark or plum jacket or suit. Hair oiled and combed. Big black boots replaced the pointed suede shoes. My unwanted and lonely trousers were flung in the wardrobe unwashed and unfolded, not even hung up. There they stayed forgotten for a long time, the suede shoes being the only companion.

Then, oh the joy... finally the trousers were raked out and rescued. I pulled them on, despite their being rather tight and short in the leg. I squeezed into them and secured the belt to stop them falling off my hips. I was clearly not the same shape anymore! The joy my trousers felt being taken out into the sun again to be admired by all. The sun shone on the yellow belt and silver buckle as they were taken for a stroll around the garden and the flares swished through the grass.

Then the trousers realised something terrible was happening. They were not free to be admired at all. They had been made into a slave to do gardening! The knees became stretched and filthy as I kneeled on the grass to weed. The hems trailed in the mud and soil and sometimes the legs were drenched in water from a hosepipe. Even worse were the sharp nails and snotty handkerchiefs pushed into the pockets. Over time the legs became ripped by thorns until finally they were thrown back into the dark wardrobe.

The strange thing is that the trousers noticed new trousers being hung in there ... and they had ripped legs too! New trousers with rips all over the legs? And made from nasty denim. The trousers now wait in the dark, bewildered and ashamed, for the day when the great seamstress in the sky will take them to the great recycling dump.

Genre: Fiction. Topic: "Time". By Helen Griffith

Time to meditate

Time and space. I seem to have spent my life so far wishing I had more of each. Conversely the older I get, the less of it I have! Take last Saturday, which was a typical day in the Johnson household. The day began at seven o'clock with my youngest Freya jumping onto the bed.

"Wake up Mummy!" she shouted in my ear. I notice that she never jumps on John who promptly rolled away from the noise and continued to snore.

Wearily, I roused myself and got dressed. No such thing as a lie-in, in this house! Hannah, our eldest, was already awake and playing with her toys in the lounge. She is always happy to play by herself and would allow me a lie-in but Freya is like my little shadow.

I was soon into the routine of breakfast and getting the girls ready for the day. Once done, I left the girls to their own devices, while I then spent a manic two hours getting the washing on, doing the breakfast dishes, watering the plants etc; the usual Saturday morning chores for a working woman.

Right! I thought to myself, I'm going to have a ten-minute meditation break whilst the house is quiet.

Freya was in her bedroom playing nicely and John had taken Hannah to gymnastics. Grabbing my meditation cushion, I made my way to the lounge. Opening the door, I was greeted by what looked like a tsunami but was in fact Hannah's toys strewn all over the floor. As usual she was late for gymnastics and had just left everything in a state of abandonment. I cleared a space and sat down.

Eyes closed, I forced myself to forget about the carnage around me and centred on my breath:
Breathing in – I am calm
Breathing out – Let go
Breathing in – I *am* calm
Breathing out – Let go!

I had just got into a steady rhythm when my right eye was peeled back by a little hand.

"Mummy, are you awake?" Freya was gazing closely into my eye, her porridge breath invading my nostrils. "I've lost Panda," she said with a whimper.

Repressing a sigh, I knew there would be no peace until the errant animal had been located. We had just found him hiding down the side of the bed when the sound of keys turning in the lock marked the return of John and Hannah. No chance now to return to the peace of five minutes ago.

I was soon into the lunchtime routine followed by a trip to town for new school shoes. As usual, there was no "me time" on a Saturday but I promised myself that I would find that much needed ten minutes later. By the time tea, bath and bedtime had been achieved, I felt quite frazzled. Time to return to that meditation!

I grabbed my cushion and opened the lounge door. The carnage of earlier had now disappeared and in its place sat my husband, feet up, pint in hand watching the rugby.

Okay, I thought, no problem. I'll just use the guest room. However, when I opened the door, I was greeted by a mountain of packaging waste that John said he would take to the tip but hadn't yet done so.

Okay. Last resort the bedroom. I took myself into our bedroom and looked around for some space. A pile of John's work clothes littered the floor and some mail order parcels were stacked in a pile in front of the wardrobe waiting for me to try them on. With a sigh, I scooped the packages up and dumped them onto the bed.

Right where was I?

Sitting on my cushion, I once again centred my breath and cleared my thoughts of all the things I still needed to do. I had done perhaps seven minutes when I was aware of the bedroom door being opened. There was my youngest, ruffled hair and panda in hand.

"Mummy, I can't get to sleep!"

"Okay, Sweetie, let's get you back to bed. Would you like a story?"

I settled Freya back into her bed and read her favourite book about Penguin Small. I then sang both her and myself to sleep. Waking sometime later and feeling decidedly groggy, I took myself back to the lounge. John was now watching *Match of the Day*, another pint in hand. Too late for any further attempts at meditation, so I turned to medication instead and opened a bottle of wine!

Genre: Poetry. Topic: "Description". By Tony Wilson

The Obelisk at Stourhead

A great house where visitors meet
the surrounding air shimmers in heat,
out of the window the visitor sees

an obelisk of stone, dividing the trees.

Tall the column rises, pierces the sky
above a grassy carpet where daisies lie,
dotted and mottled with yellow and blue
and leafy greens of every hue.

A resplendent face atop the obelisk bold
reflects the Sun in burnished gold,
Latin text encircles its girth
tells of its creator, his right of birth

but insects, birds, grasses, flowers
tell of another in daylit hours,
their great creator, their right of birth,
the creator of all, the creator of Earth.

Genre: Non-fiction. Topic: "Time". By Jan Mills

The good old days?

> "I miss the good old days"
> "Life was so much simpler then, so much better"
> "How things have changed over time".

How often do I hear these sentiments from people of my own generation and the one before. How often do I feel this myself – slower, simpler, better?

I close my eyes and the years slide away – fifty plus years – more than half a century. Is that really possible? I am a student nurse again, starting my psychiatric nurse training. I'm young, enthusiastic and on the first rung of my chosen career.

The hospital is huge – a maze of long, soulless corridors leading to endless wards home to thirty-forty patients. I use the term "the hospital" loosely; it is a true institution – a "community home", but for most patients it was a permanent "home" with a laundry, hairdresser, school, shop and so on. The Ward Sisters and Charge Nurses were self-appointed "gods" ruling their own unique kingdoms. That made it very difficult if one took a fancy to a young student nurse! Their power was absolute and I developed numerous strategies for dealing with the wandering hands of a senior nurse or extricating myself from being pinned against the store cupboard wall whilst still smiling and keeping my "attacker" in good humour. I had friends on other wards who would warn me when a certain Nursing Officer was on the prowl, so I could make my way to a public place! Better times? Hmm…

The life of many of the long-term patients was not happy or fulfilling. There was no personal choice. If someone did not want to take their medication it would be disguised in food or given forcefully. Shades of "One Flew Over the Cuckoo's Nest!" When I began my training, the major anti-psychotics had just become available – Chlorpromazine and its derivatives and these were used liberally to "manage" patients. Still, I guess this was better than the drug they replaced – Paraldehyde, once smelled, never forgotten. This was given in a glass syringe because it would melt the plastic ones! Better times? Hmm…

ECT, (electro-convulsive therapy) was widely used. I know it is still used today but my memories of the treatment I remember are very different – barbaric. Four staff would hold the patient's arms and legs to control the violent spasms as electric shocks were administered, (muscle relaxants were still drugs of the future). The hard rubber gag stopped the person biting their tongue. This treatment did help some people come through the suicidal phase quicker in depression but, the resultant loss of memory and personality was a high price to pay. One lady, Joan, was so severely depressed and such a high suicide risk, it was decided she would benefit from a prefrontal leucotomy. After surgery she learned to walk – well, shuffle, but never used words again. She was incontinent and needed help to eat. She was forty-five years old; had been a teacher with children and grandchildren. She was now an empty shell. Better times? Hmm...

Slipping through time and it is now 1988. I have three young children and am working a sixty-hour week. My husband does not like working and has aspirations to be a house-husband, without the housework! I thought that people in psychiatric hospitals had little choice. It is even worse in a hospital for people with learning disabilities – the language has changed – the practices have not. This hospital has mostly male patients, there is one ward with ladies and one mixed ward. A number of the ladies have been there since they were teenagers. They were admitted for being pregnant out of wedlock (diagnosis of being an "idiot with loose morals"), and in many cases this was caused by the assault of a male family member or friend. Better times? Hmm...

Bath-time in the morning was a very public affair – men lined up in wheelchairs or on commodes wheeled into the bathroom, were undressed and bathed in one of three baths in the open-plan bathroom, usually by young female care staff with no curtains for privacy. The thirty beds in the dormitory were separated only by lockers. Bundles were made up the night before: elasticated trousers, bri-nylon jumpers, shirts and underwear taken from the linen cupboard – stock clothes of mixed shapes, colours and sizes, shared randomly. They were lucky to get a matching pair of socks! People only wore their own clothes when they were due a family visit. And yet these men had £1000s in their bank accounts. Better times? Hmm...

The practices I saw, and went to great lengths to change, were by no means unusual. During the 1970s and 80s there were several instances of:"scandal of exposed abuse in mental handicap hospitals". The abuse was verbal, physical, financial, sexual and neglect and had been perpetrated over many years and often decades. (Ely, Frome etc.) In the most extreme cases there were reports of non-accidental death. Each time there was an outcry and people said: "this must never happen again". But people with special support needs have always been persecuted for their differentness. I would like to think that now with personalisation and the focus on care packages based on assessment, that supporting individual needs would eradicate such cruelty. But the latest programme I saw on TV depicting abuse in a learning disability care environment was only a few years ago.

Times may change the language and the prescribed practices but it doesn't change the hearts of people!

Genre: Non-Fiction. Topic: "Ancient". By Ted Mason

YanMen Pass

In the ancient YanMen Pass, in the North of Shanxi Province there are, as in many parts of China, trees said to be thousands of years old, often propped up in temples like gnarled and crippled old men. In Dai Xian County one such tree is said to have once shaded Confucius as he instructed his followers, and as a tiny sapling it may have witnessed great scholars, poets and Generals taking rest there on the way to the garrison city of DaTong. This was a huge fortified military city with stables and barracks for a thousand horses and thousands of troops. Now it is a modern city mostly built outside its original walls, attracting

Chinese tourists to admire its walls and military history.

To the South is Beijing, previously Peking, once home of the Emperor and his Forbidden City. North West of the city the Great Wall straddles the contours of the hills from the Shanhai Pass in the East to Jiayu Pass in the West. Built over 2,000 years by five dynasties of Emperors to protect Peking from the Mongols, it is high enough not to be climbed and wide enough to allow five horses to trot abreast along its battlements. At regular intervals the wall is supported by small forts along its length, the largest being at places where the wall has fortified gates blocking passes between hills. These were the gateways to Mongolia. Many great battles were fought at one such pass. It is called the YanMen or Juyong pass. This is one of the nearest gateways to Peking, between Inner Mongolia and Shanxi. To lose this gate would mean the loss of the Chinese Dynasty to the Mongol hoards. Four Generals from one noble family died here protecting the gate. It is said that one soldier would be able to hold the gate against 1,000 Mongols!

The revered old tree may remember them, being even now a focus for Buddhist prayer and thanks. It could have witnessed General Li Chonghui leading battalions of troops shuffling along the mud road to the wall. There would have been miles of flag-waving cavalry with peasant farmers running behind, collecting horse dung to spread on their fields; all this blood to nourish Chinese soil and the Mongolian grasslands beyond the great gate. Along its length most of the wall remains; some restored but much still overgrown, in disrepair and dangerous to climb.

From the battlements that are open to tourists, there are three views once witnessed by soldiers. Look north out across the Mongolian Steps where once Mongolian horsemen would gather on the grasslands to gaze in wonder at the huge wall. To the West the soldiers on duty would see the wall and its defences rising up and sloping down the contours of the hills. At dusk the wall would be golden in the setting sun, turning to red as fires were lit along its length. South would stretch fields of crops criss-crossed with mud highways and dotted with brown and grey peasant houses. Far on the horizon the garrisons of DaTong would light up the sky with fires.

Now in old age, the ancient tree sleeps happily as it knows a new YanMen Pass. The man-made walls have crumbled to nothing, or have been stolen to build little villages straddling the highway winding south. The great gate has rotted into the soil or perhaps burned as firewood. It is now only a gap between two ridges of grass covered soil. Wild flowers grow where once enormous stone blocks formed the base of the wall. A very few smiling Chinese tourists walk freely through the pass into the green grasslands of Mongolia. Some climb to the top of the ridge to take photos, and all imagine what a glorious and powerful sight it must have been a thousand years ago.But there are more interesting photos to take further West where the winding wall is strong and the views more spectacular. Only a small white minibus waits for them beyond a field of barley. Perhaps it will take them further East, where a restored section of the wall is accessed by tourists from Beijing. There is no gate there. They will soon forget the YanMen Pass.

The old tree smiles as the intruders all leave. Nature and peace are returning. The last to go is a little girl with a red bow in her long jet-black hair who stoops down to pick a yellow flower growing between two small blocks of stone. A warm breeze rustles over the grassland and the dry crops, and the ancient tree rests.

Genre: Aide Memoire. Topic: "Success". By Alan Pearce

Universal "Thank You/Sorry" letter

(This is a "thank you" letter pro-forma for all occasions for lazy recipients of hospitality who nevertheless know that a "thank you" letter has to be written. Simply fill it in as necessary and delete what does not apply.)

Address......................................

Date..............

Dear............. and/or..............

I write to thank you very much indeed for your very kind hospitality on....................
 I particularly enjoyed the food/beef/pork/ham/veal/venison and the booze/drink/choice of wine that accompanied it, champagne/coffee and also thesinging/dancing/bluemovies/snogging that followed it. I really must thank you in particular for your offer of a loan/an alibi/tomato plants/unpaid employment/chocolates to take home/an invitation to your investiture/transport to the political rally/joining your swingers' group/help with the police enquiries/assistance with the stuck trouser zip/daughter's hand in marriage/sponsorship to the National Front/unblocking my lavatory next weekend/advice on a vasectomy/ and also the crutches/long talk on the subject of bunions/foreign postage stamps/slug pellets/equine VD/flatus incidents you have experienced.

I was surprised to hear about the poor holiday/death of your young pet rat/transvestite relationship/melting of the tar on your road/the Mothers Union Bomb Making Group/dodgy plumber/cost of cheese in Waitrose/Convent of the Little Sisters of Peace and Mercy Total Retribution society/infestation in the bedroom/collapse of the vintage motorbike restoration club/your dislike of cricket/the Rastafarians next door.

I am very sorry that I collapsed/didn't notice you new hair style/mistook your bidet for a WC/was sick on your dog/used the "f" word/didn't make it clear that my medical condition could be infectious/insulted your maid/broke the antique glass table mat/ flashed at your neighbour/didn't pay sufficient attention to your wallpaper/husband/wife/dog/cactus/advances.

I am so grateful that you washed my shirt/revived me before the Loyal Toast/laughed at my jokes/called the ambulance/forgave me for the vibrator incident/want to see me again/didn't tell anybody about "you know what"/took me home/have still got a sense of humour.

You and your husband/wife/partner/co-habitee/lodger/cat were particularly open/kind/busty/non-judgemental/sweaty/keento know of the whereabouts of my warts/thankful that I left, for which I am also grateful/responsible/liable/repentant.

I really liked your beautiful table flowers but with hindsight I know I shouldn't have eaten them. Please forgive me for this and for anything else I may have left out.

Yours very sincerely,

....

Genre: Fiction. Topic: "Law".By Barbara Shea

Little Georgie Brown

The rabbits were dead anyway. That made them easier to steal than the live ones in their wicker cages on the next stall. Even so, it was a difficult task and needed careful planning.

We eventually decided that Mary would cause a distraction in the street by screaming and accusing a passing stranger of trying to molest her. She was only six years old, but clever at acting and, with a bit of practice, I felt she would do well. My part was more difficult. Whilst she was screaming and causing a disturbance, I had to pull the rabbits from their hooks, hide them under my large, ill-fitting coat and disappear into the crowd.

Easier said than done. When it came to it, Mary didn't scream loudly enough and people continued to hurry by without taking any notice. I decided to carry on anyway. We were desperate. Our dad had disappeared on one of his benders (that's alcoholic binges to you) and our mum was sick and couldn't work. There was no food left and we had to do something. I thought I'd got away with it and had grabbed the rabbits when suddenly someone shouted "It's the Law", and I heard the whistles and rattles of the Bow Street Runners. I was seized by the collar squirming and kicking, with arms flailing, I was hauled off. I could see Mary running away. To cut a long story short, I was taken before the Magistrate and sentenced to two months' hard labour in Oxford Gaol.

It was just as bad as I had imagined. Filth was everywhere, prisoners were wailing and crying and the cell was packed with people either sitting or lying on the floor. The stench was dreadful with so many unwashed bodies lying together, but the nights were the worst thing. Although the heat could be stifling during the day, at night it was freezing cold and that's when the rats came out. They would nibble anything they thought they could eat, including us, and I didn't dare go to sleep. It wasn't only the rats I feared. Some of the other prisoners could be violent. The only relief, if you can call it that, was when we were allowed to leave the cell for work. My job was the Shot Drill. This involved lifting a heavy iron cannon ball, bringing it up slowly until it was level with my chest and carrying it three steps to my right, putting it down and then repeating the task with another cannon ball. Pointless, exhausting and humiliating. One thing it did though was build up my muscles.

One day a new pile of rags appeared in the cell. By that, I mean another human being. Beneath these rags was an old man of around fifty. As I peered more closely at him, I realised that I recognised him. The other street boys and thieves had referred to him with some respect as "The Governor". I kicked him and he stirred. He looked up at me with bleary eyes and a slow smile spread across his face.

"Well," he said, "If it ain't little Georgie Brown, all growed up! What you doing in here?"

I related the sad story of the rabbits and how I ended up in gaol, and to my surprise, he laughed.

"You want to be more careful," he said, the grin still on his face. "I'd never let meself be caught like that."

"And yet" I replied "here you are."

"Well, that was just a little misunderstanding between me and the Magistrate. I think I must be losing me touch. I know all the Beaks and usually have something on them.I just have to remind them of their little peccadilloes and they let me off. Unfortunately, Mr Justice Walker seems to live a very pure Christian life and didn't take kindly to the likes of me suggesting otherwise."

I grinned. It seemed a very long time since someone had made me smile. Then he said something interesting. "Well, boy, how would you like to learn to thieve properly?"

Over the course of the next few nights, when neither of us could sleep, he told me all he knew about stealing and, just in case I was caught, about the various magistrates, their vices and how to blackmail them without it appearing obvious. By the time I left prison, I was well versed in the art of thievery, blackmail and extortion and well placed to share this knowledge with the rest of my family and the wider community.

I'm now doing quite nicely for myself. They say crime doesn't pay, but I beg to differ, and prison certainly works – or at least it did for me!

Genre: Fiction. Topic: "Airport". By Jan Mills

The Airport

It is time, at last! Here we are, at the airport, sitting in the executive lounge. Well, why not indulge in a little extra luxury? We have waited so long and this is such a momentous trip; the final lap of our journey. We have spent months planning this – nine months to be precise. We have read every brochure and book about our destination; we have listened to so many of our friends' accounts we can hardly wait to get there. We have even attended classes to learn about where we are going – the language, the pitfalls and risks to be avoided, what you should and should not do. We now feel ready as we take these last steps, so we know what to expect. We have packed all the right clothes, and we have the right currency. We are so excited; a bit scared but full of an overwhelming sense of anticipation and hope as we board the plane that will take us to the wonderful, warm, sunny beach resort in Mauritius.

We look around the plane and recognise a few faces and nod and smile at each other. We hold each other's hand as we take off and although there are a number of bumps on the flight it is much as we expected. We sense the plane circling, before coming in to land. We squeeze hands as we imagine alighting in blazing heat. The pilot's voice comes out loud through the speakers: "Ladies and Gentlemen, welcome to Alaska!"

We look around in confusion. The other passengers are doing the same. We haven't booked to fly to Alaska! We have the wrong clothes, the wrong money, all the wrong expectations. How could this happen? What will we do? How will we manage?

In doubt and confusion, we shuffle down the airplane steps and walk hesitantly into the arrivals lounge. No one comes to greet us, to show us where to go or what to do. We look shamefacedly at the other passengers. They, too, look dejected, avoiding making eye contact with others. Some couples cling together, others pull apart, unable to cope with the different place to which they had come. The airport staff look sympathetic, but don't look directly at us – they are embarrassed, they don't know what to say and when we ask for directions, they just shrug.

It takes a long time to find our way around our new destination: to learn the language, to understand the culture; mostly we find our way by making mistakes and learning from those. Sometimes we have support from our fellow passengers. Gradually, we learn to love "Alaska"; there are so many unexpected joyful moments as we begin to accept that this is where we are. Sometimes we think wistfully about the warm and sunny shores we had expected but when we look into the face of our beautiful baby daughter, we know that we would not change where we are for anywhere else in the world! Our little Mia has Down's Syndrome and is everything to us.

Genre:Fiction.   Topic: "Memories".By   Helen Griffith

Memories

I tentatively swing open the garden gate and am immediately hit by an assault on my senses. My nose is bombarded with a heady fragrance; my eyes a cacophony of colour. The roses sway in the gentle breeze, glistening with the tears from a late summer shower. It was as if nothing had changed and yet everything had.

I pause and unbidden tears well up in my eyes. What might have been!

Giving myself a shake, I pull myself together and set off down the garden to see if the bench, our bench, still exists. The bottom of the garden is now overgrown with weeds and I nearly miss the little path that will take me to the hill-top with glorious westerly views over the English Channel. I make my way slowly past stinging nettles and brambles, vying with each other for territory, until I find the clearing. The bench is still there, hanging on for dear life, ravaged over time. I sit down and look out to sea. It is impossible to be here and not to think about that summer of '76…

Mum was ill and thus it was decided that we three girls would spend the summer holidays with various relatives. For me, that meant a whole summer with my cousin, Susan. She and Auntie Margery lived in a small thatched cottage by the sea in Kent, which meant that Susan and I spent many happy hours wandering the sea shore or going into the local town. I had often stayed with them during the summer but this summer was different as Susan had discovered boys! Well actually, one boy in particular, Mark. She could hardly contain her excitement to tell me all about him. He was in the sixth form and went to the same youth club as her. She planned to make him notice her by becoming a brilliant table tennis player so that they could become doubles partners.

This plan failed but because they now had a common interest, Mark had noticed her and on the third week of my holidays, asked her out to the cinema. Susan was beside herself, her first proper date! When her mother insisted that I came too, Mark invited his best friend Sanjay to make up a foursome.

As the summer progressed, Susan and Mark's relationship blossomed and Sanjay and I often found ourselves thrown together by default. Sanjay was the complete opposite to Mark; very quiet and unassuming. I think he hadn't had much to do with white girls up to now but over the weeks, we gradually got to know each other better and spent hours talking about the differences in our upbringing, religions and cultures. Though we came from different worlds we found lots in common and became firm friends.

The summer holiday flew by and in no time at all it was my last day. I had arranged to meet Sanjay on the hilltop so we could say goodbye in private. Secretly, I was hoping that he would kiss me. I was full of anticipation as I entered the rose garden and made my way up the path towards the bench. As I rounded the last corner, I saw that Sanjay was already there, gazing out over the glistening water. I sat next to him and for a moment both of us were lost in the sight of the sunsetting; light glimmering over the sea towards us. In faltering words, Sanjay explained how his parents had already lined up an Indian girl for him to marry. He felt he could not go against his parents by having an open relationship with me. All he could really offer me was a covert and long-distance friendship.

I was devastated; I wasn't interested in friendship! What was the point? I tried to stop the emotions showing on my face and it was all that I could do to stumble out some platitudes and bid him farewell. Abruptly, I turned and ran towards the house, tears streaming from my eyes.

My reveries are disturbed by a robin struggling to pull a worm out of the ground. As I watch the little bird, I wonder what would have happened if we had taken the relationship further. I contemplate how the world has changed since that summer; how I have changed. With a clarity of vision, I understand that our friendship formed a fundamental part in who I am today and what I value in life. I silently thank Sanjay for the time we spent together and then I slip back through the garden to my own world.

Genre: Flash fiction and microfiction. By Various

"Flash fiction" is a very short story, "microfiction" is an extremely short story. The aim is to be evocative in as few words as possible.

Flash fiction (examples)

Len and Mary were Yorkshire born and bred. Mary died. Len got the stonemason to put "Lord, she was Thine" on his very religious wife's headstone.

He went to see the finished article. It said: "Lord, she was Thin".

He expostulated: "You've left the "E" off!"

The stonemason replied "Luk. Don't lose tha rag!" (He was Yorkshire, too.) "It goes on the end – Ah can fit it in easy like. Cum back tomorrer."

Len returned. To his horror it now said: "Eee Lord, she was Thin". (86 words).

Two beech trees stand tall together.
Branches link arm in arm.
Their nuts litter the fertile ground
Who now can tell which tree they are from?

Early seedlings struggle, finding space to grow
So, in years ahead, they too
May caress another's branches
And sway in the warm west wind. (50 words).

The little boy was allowed to attend the first course of his parents' dinner party, "for the experience". His Mummy said "Say Grace for us, Dear."

He said he didn't know what to say. His Mummy replied: "You remember what Daddy said at lunch? It begins with 'O God'".

"Are you sure, Mummy?"

"Yes, Dear."

"I still don't understand one of the words..."

"Just start, Dear."

The little boy put his hands together, looked up to the heavens, and said: "O God, it's tonight those excruciating people are coming round for supper!" (92 words)

Microfiction(examples)

I breed cats. The shop had one in the window: "Royal Netherlands White". If pedigree, worth a fortune; if a cross, pet value only. I asked the shopkeeper the obvious question – which is...? * (33 words)(See * after next piece for answer.)

My wife was in labour. I was in the waiting room. A kind nurse, making coffee, leaned out of a door and said: "Did you want black or white?" I fainted. (31 words)

"You don't have to say anything, but anything you do say will be noted and may be used against you."
"I know. I'm married." (24 words)

Lever pulled. Trapdoor opened. Last vision.Rider reprieve. (8 words)

"San Andreas, they're saying it's all your fault." (8 words)

The cannibals barely ate their food. (6 words)

"You're wrong, Vlad." (3 words)

"Boris. No." (2 words)

Microfiction(answer)

* First clue: How important was it that the cat was pedigree?
* Second clue: What is the adjective for something coming from the Netherlands?
* Third clue: What is another word for "cat" (slang)?
* Fourth clue: Where was the cat?
* Answer: "How Dutch is that moggy in the window?"

Genre: Fiction.Topic: "Danger". By Carol Waterkeyn

The lost diary

I was having a bad day. I was thinking how becoming a widow was hard work. First there was the inquest, getting the death certificate, then the funeral to arrange. After that, the reading of the Will and all that endless paperwork and clearing out when you were supposed to be spending time grieving was almost too much to bear.

I was just emptying out Eric's wardrobe when the phone rang. I dropped the black plastic sack and rubber gloves onto the floor and went to answer it.

"Is that Mrs Waters?" asked this rough voice.

"Yes, speaking," I replied.

"You don't know me but I must speak wiv you urgent," he said.

"Well, I hope you are not trying to sell me anything!" Since Eric died, I've had no end of people trying to sell me double-glazing, kitchens, alarms – and it's always the same, pushy people who won't take no for an answer.

"No, I'm not tryin' to sell you anyfin'," the man said.

"Well, what's this about? Who are you?" Frankly I was getting impatient.

"You can call me Albert, and it's more about what I can do for *you.* Have you got a red diary?"

"Er, yes…go on."

"You did have a diary, but now I've got it. 'Found it in M&S's car park."

I'd been shopping there that morning. I'd wanted to buy a few nice things to cheer myself up and I was fed up with wearing all that black clothing. I must have dropped the diary when I was looking for my car keys and trying to hold all the bags at once.

I told him: "It's very good of you to ring me. Can you post it to the address inside the cover?" I was grateful.

"I fink it would be safer if I brought it 'round. You see I've bin reading it. Couldn't help meself. It's rather hot stuff if yer don't mind me sayin', all those steamy times you had with your lover, Mrs Waters.

Then I remembered reading in the paper about a Mr Waters who died recent-like. Accident wiv a garden hose, wasn't it? Tripped and banged his 'ead? I fink the police would be very interested to read yer diary and about this other man yer've been seein'. 'Course if you make it worth me while I'll let you have it back and we'll say no more about it."

I gathered my thoughts. This man could make things very awkward, very awkward indeed.

"Oy, are you still there?" growled the voice.

"Yes, maybe you'd better come round after all. Can you come tonight?"

"Hah, I thought you'd see sense, Missus."

"Okay, how does five hundred pounds sound as a reward for the diary? Not that I've done anything wrong you understand."

"Two fousand would sound better!"

"And where do you expect me to get that sort of money from? And blackmail is against the law, you know."

"From the insurance yer husband had, I imagine."

"Oh alright, two thousand it is. Shall we say seven o'clock?"

I put the receiver down and picked up my rubber gloves, to carry on with clearing out the wardrobe. Then, through gritted teeth, I thought it would make a good temporary receptacle for a body. I'd got away with one murder, so another shouldn't be too difficult. Plus, if anyone found out I could say he was an intruder and that he'd tried to attack me knowing I was a defenceless widow, that I panicked and didn't know what to do whilst the balance of my mind was disturbed through grieving. Then I would be safe, and in time, the lovely Patrick and I could move away, buy a super place on the continent with the insurance money and live happily ever after.

The hours ticked away slowly until it was time for my visitor. Everything was ready. The kitchen knife was hidden in the drawer of the hall table. I removed the mirror from the wall so that the blackmailer wouldn't be able to see my reflection when I crept up on him. I'd keep him in the hall in a confined space so he couldn't get away. The adrenaline was pumping. I was on a high and would have the advantage of surprise.

There was just one problem. The man *had* told the police about the diary and they were listening in on the phone conversation. The guy who arrived at seven was a plain-clothed policeman. He handed me the diary, then grabbed my arm as the knife came towards him.

After two constables burst through the door and restrained me, he said: "Ruth Waters. I am charging you with the murder of Eric Waters and attacking a police officer. You are not obliged to say anything, but anything you do say may be used in evidence against you later in court."

I felt faint, had a heart attack and now I'm in the hospital with a female police constable sitting next to me. Patrick's done a bunk, the swine, leaving me to face the music.

Genre: Non-fiction. Topic: "Retribution". By Alan Pearce

Snowman

Beating aside the heavy snow and biting wind, the huge aircraft carrier slid its way into Portsmouth harbour through the narrow entrance, with Portsmouth's Still and West public house overhanging the water to the right and Gosport's Fort Blockhouse to the left. The tugs carefully guided it to its berth, like a feral mother shepherding her offspring to safety in the wintry weather. The wires and storm hawsers were lowered fore, aft and midships and the vessel was secured to the huge Victorian iron and concrete bollards, which had been taking the strain of battleships, cruisers and now aircraft carriers for as long as they had existed. She was now safe in her winter berth and the crew could take Christmas leave.

Which they did. Almost straight away. By the end of the day three quarters of the ship's company had streamed down the gangways and set off for the bosom of their families, leaving behind just those who had lost the "Christmas leave ballot" to shut things down for the forthcoming hibernation.

This "duty watch" had little to do except for carrying out "rounds" to check for safety, and practising fire drills. But in their spare time several of them built a large snowman at the foot of the gangway – traditional, with carrot and coal but also sporting a jolly sailor's cap and a blue sailor's collar and holding a brightly coloured placard which said: "Welcome to our ship. Merry Christmas!" It all seemed very cosy and homely.

At 5pm the dockyard hooter signalled the end of the working day and the workers set off for the gates. But one of them had a car and was giving a lift to several others. On the way out, this carload of dockyard workers spotted the snowman, veered off the feeder road, drove straight into it at speed and smashed it to smithereens. They drove off, laughing.

The sailors diligently and lugubriously rebuilt the snowman, a bit further along the road. The following day, scenting more fun, the car returned for more sport and smashed the new snowman to bits.

It was carefully and laboriously rebuilt again, just a little further along the road. There was a slight difference on this occasion, however. The sailors built their third snowman round one of the huge Victorian iron and concrete bollards at the side of the road. At 5pm the car appeared again... I think you can finish this story for yourself.

Revenge, as they say, is a dish best served cold. Retribution it was.

Genre: Non-Fiction. Topic: "Sense". By Barbara Shea

Hearing

I'd like to tell you about my grandmother. Her name was Annie Edeson and she was born in 1884. One of six siblings, all of whom suffered hearing loss of varying degrees, her hearing was impaired from the age of three.

As a child, I remember visiting her in the 1960s with my cousin Susan, who was the same age as myself. Annie, in common with other deaf ladies of her era, used to sew pockets into her blouses to hold the huge hearing aid battery. Unfortunately, she and her closest sister Edith insisted on turning the hearing aids off in order to save the batteries. Since neither sister could hear, conversations were often amusing and sometimes downright bizarre! When the hearing aids were eventually turned on, they would whistle and pop if not tuned correctly, and the family often wondered if she could pick up the BBC on them. Annie and Edith of course, could hear nothing of the whistling. Whilst it was extremely painful for the rest of us, they remained in blissful ignorance.

Annie was a very religious lady, which meant that there was no music other than hymn singing allowed on a Sunday, and the only books she would allow us to read had to be of an improving nature.

Amazingly, although deaf, she was able to hold a hymn tune perfectly; in fact, far better than Susan and myself, who had voices sounding like frogs in a box!

When my cousin and I visited, Annie and Edith would frequently break wind, particularly after Sunday lunch. Being hard of hearing, they were oblivious to the effect it was having on everyone else and this resulted in Susan and myself being sent from the room on many occasions, as we couldn't control our laughter. Typically childish behaviour but Annie and Edith were always puzzled by the fact that we were doubled up with laughter and consequently banished.

When my parents celebrated their silver wedding anniversary, Annie, along with other family and friends, was invited to the party at a local hotel. There was a band and dancing, which I always thought must have seemed very strange since she couldn't hear the music and would just have seen lots of bodies gyrating silently and not particularly elegantly. It must have looked like a scene from Dante's Inferno! By this time, my attitude towards her deafness had taken a much more compassionate turn and I'd started to think about how hard life must have been for her and how strange it would be to live in a world without sound.

Now that I'm in my seventies I know several people who wear hearing aids — minute things which are unobtrusive and discreet and, amazingly, can be linked to mobile phones. How wonderful that we live in an age where deafness can be overcome to a certain extent with the aid of technology – and that the rest of us no longer have to listen to the whistling and popping of other people's hearing aids!

Genre: Fiction. Topic: "Danger". By Jan Mills

Crystal ball

"Go on, Charlie," nudged her friend, Caro, "give it a try."

"I don't believe in all that mumbo-jumbo," Charlie scoffed, "Madame Zaza in a headscarf, hooped earrings and long flowing skirt, rings on every finger, looking into her crystal ball and telling me I will meet a tall, dark, handsome stranger!"

"Go on," Caro urged, "I'll pay!"

Charlie gave in, as usual. It was always impossible to say "no" to Caro; she was a real force to be reckoned with. They were as different as chalk and cheese. Caro was petite, dark haired, with a fiery temper and a spiky tongue. Charlie was fair, quite tall, willowy with a gentle nature, or as Caro said, she was a "pushover".

The girls entered the booth, surprised to see a very ordinary looking woman sitting on an easy chair opposite a two-seater settee; no sign of tea cups, tarot cards or a crystal ball anywhere.

"Come, sit." Her voice though soft, had a compelling cadence and Charlie found herself moving to sit on the settee opposite her.

"I am Andre," she said, her eyes fixed on Charlie's. As she held out her hands Charlie placed hers in them. Caro, who was really not used to being ignored at all started to speak, but Andre silenced her with a look. Andre looked into Charlie's eyes and frowned. "There is an aura around you; I sense the danger from an unexpected source. It is not clear. You need to be alert, to follow your own instincts and not allow yourself to be swayed by another."

As they left the booth, Caro was loudly sceptical: "What a load of hooey!"

A few weeks later Caro turned up at Charlie's house: "C'mon, we're going to that new club."

"Sorry," said Charlie: "I'm going out with Rob. He's asked me out at last!"

"Great", said Caro, "Where are we going? I'll bring Phil."

"It's my first date with Rob; I think he wants it to be just us," said Charlie, "he's taking me to that new Italian Restaurant, Toscana."

"You shouldn't be on your own with him, you don't really know him," countered Caro. "I'll come along with Phil."

Charlie tried a few times to put Caro off, but to no avail.

Caro and Phil had turned up early and were already there when Rob and Charlie arrived. Rob looked put out and was quite silent throughout the meal. Not that it mattered, Caro talked enough for all of them.

A fortnight later Caro turned up just as Charlie was getting into a taxi. She wouldn't tell Caro where she was going, so she just said she was meeting Rob, alone. Caro was not happy and she decided to follow the taxi. When she walked into the bar where Charlie and Rob were huddled in a cosy booth, she went straight up to them.

"Fancy seeing you two here!" With skin like a rhino, she plonked herself beside them and sat there for the next hour. It was too much for Rob, who couldn't take another five minutes of her self-centred chatter. He banged his glass on the table, grunted "goodnight" and left abruptly.

A week later, Charlie and Rob were walking along the local stony beach. It was such a relief to be on their own, with a chance to get away from Caro and start to learn a little about each other. Suddenly they heard shouts from behind them.

"Hey, wait for me."

Rob shouted at Caro – she was not welcome; why could she not leave him and Charlie alone? He wanted to spend some time on his own with Charlie.

Caro shouted back that he was trying to isolate Caro from her friends and family; why did he want her alone?

As Caro continued to shout accusations at Rob he stopped: "I give in, go on with your girlfriend!" And with that, he stormed back down the beach to his car, and drove off.

Charlie was in tears and Caro made all the right sympathetic noises.

"He wasn't right for you. Thank God you found out about him now. Why did he keep insisting on being alone with you? You don't know what he might have done if I hadn't come along to save you – remember what the fortune teller said."

"Do you really think he was a risk to me?" sobbed Charlie, "he seemed so nice!"

"Mark my words", said Caro, "he wanted to separate you from your friends and manipulate you."

Caro bundled Charlie into the car and she started back along the cliff road. She was chuckling to herself as she drove; congratulating herself on how clever she had been to prise Charlie away from Rob. She did not see the "Danger" sign warning that the cliff edge was eroding. She was still chuckling as the car hit a pile of rough stones where the kerb used to be.

She was still chuckling as the car left the road and sailed over the edge of the cliff…

Genre: Non-Fiction. Topic: "Space". By Ted Mason

Space

We inhabit a strange and wonderful planet. Viewed from our moon it is sapphire amidst the blackness of a space be-speckled with tiny diamonds. But to a creature from another planet, we may only be a source of food and minerals. Here, we are arrogant enough to believe we are better than other inhabitants of this world, even though our intelligence is limited and only small portions of our brains are used. Consider the existence of other creatures on this planet over time. A species does not need much intelligence to survive and prosper. Dinosaurs, insects and birds lived here for millions of years.

Dinosaurs survived for so long because they killed and foraged within their own small area. Their world was their immediate surroundings. To them the world was small. It was just a place to eat and breed. Death kept their population in balance with the natural resources around them. It took a natural disaster to wipe them out; except for crocodiles, insects, birds and fish that could range over wider distances for food.

Consider the smallest of creatures; insects. They have existed for even longer. Yet a worker ant has no plan. It wanders around haphazardly. It has no hope, but relies on pure luck to find what it needs for the colony. The colony relies on huge numbers of ants to improve the odds and prosper. To an ant the world is vast. If an ant was intelligent the sheer enormity of its habitat would be as unimaginable as our view of the universe.

Unlike the dinosaur or an insect, humans have only evolved here over a very tiny amount of time. With our small amount of intelligence, we have brought what we need to us instead of randomly searching for it. We have farms, factories and power stations, and we rely on science to continue our existence. We live longer as a result. To us this Earth used to be a huge place of oceans and mysterious lands over the horizon. Now it is a small place, not able to support a growing population. It should therefore be clear that humans face extinction unless population is reduced to correct the imbalance between human needs and the planet's available resources. Experiments with rats show that over-population with limited food creates violence and cannibalism, or disease and death. The physicist Stephen Hawking concludes that our survival depends on finding "Lebensraum" on other planets!

Humans have always killed to survive. Our greed for resources is boundless. Europeans regarded people from other cultures as heathens to be converted, enslaved and killed. Such ideas continue to this day. There is little doubt that should we expand our territory to other planets in the Milky Way, this trend would continue with their indigenous creatures. Is it not inconceivable that inhabitants of other planets might look upon the Earth similarly as a source of food, slaves and wealth. Would they recognise, admire and preserve the beauty of our planet; its oceans, art, music and culture?

There are trillions of stars in our galaxy and billions of galaxies. In each galaxy are zillions of planets. It is certain that many hundreds of thousands of planets are out there able to sustain life. Thousands of these could have created and evolved creatures far more intelligent and technologically advanced than us. With telescopes located outside our atmosphere we can see other suns as they were billions of years ago. Just as we look out into the universe, they could be briefly looking at us, dismissing their findings as insignificant. From their perspective we are of less worth than dinosaurs or insects; tiny, primitive and as boring as particles of dust. From their point of view, we might be regarded as a meat supply just as we regard cattle, or a dinosaur would have regarded its next meal!

Like the ant's view of its environment, from our point of view the size of the Universe is too large to comprehend. Are our own sizes, and the size of our planet, important factors in our survival?

We have been sending messages of greeting and peace out into the vast distances of space for many years.

Suppose that by chance such a message entered a wormhole to a galaxy unimaginably far away. Vastly more intelligent and advanced creatures on a union of planets might wrongly translate our message to mean:

"You are disgusting parasites that we will exterminate and eat!"

In anger and fear they assemble the largest fleet of warships ever seen. Their scientists retrace the origin of the signal and hyper-leap through the wormhole to appear above our atmosphere. They are surprised that there are no planetary defences and cautiously descend into the cover of a vast green forest of tall trees to prepare their invasion. There, they are cut to pieces by a lawn-mower!

In conclusion, size is as important as intelligence when examining a planet. How a planet is viewed depends on the values and needs, and intentions of the viewer.

Genre: Fiction.   Topic: "Memories".   By Viv Gough

Arthur and Michael

Arthur came here every year on his birthday.

He bent down from his wheelchair to brush away the dead leaves and remembered.

The whine shrilled to a crescendo above them and drove shrapnel, mud and wooden splinters around the trench. The whistle blew and those who had survived the blast swarmed up the ladders and over the top into no-man's land like an army of ants after the main meal.

Arthur looked for his fellow Private, Michael, in the congested struggle to move forward. Michael's eyes found his and they recognised the fear in each other.

"Keep with me, Arthur. We'll be alright if we stick together."

"I've lost you," yelled Arthur. "The smoke is so thick. Where are you?" His stomach churned and panic rose as he ran blindly onwards. Bullets sang past his ears, shells continued to burst around and the animal screams of men meeting bayonets bore into his soul.

"It's okay. I've got you," shouted Michael as he found the scruff of Arthur's collar and pulled him down into a shell crater. "We'll move forward as soon as you've calmed down a bit. Stay strong Arthur. I promise I won't leave you."

They held each other tightly and Michael gently stroked the mud and slime away from his friend's face. A thunderous blast covered them once more in filthy mud.

"I can't stand this anymore," sobbed Arthur. "I can't stop shivering and want to go home. I *must* go home."

Before Michael could grab him, Arthur ran, back towards their own trenches. Michael chased after him and pulled him down as they reached the relative safety of their own line. They lay on the swampy floor, crying and shaking. Arthur clung onto Michael who desperately pulled Arthur's face to his and kissed him.

A year before, the posters at home had gone up; proclaiming: "Your Country Needs You!" and Michael and Arthur had been swept along on a tide of patriotism. Excited, laughing and boisterous, this was their chance to escape dreary life below stairs at the big house. Michael, at twenty, was senior houseboy, dark and beautiful. Arthur, a lowly, shy, boot-boy of fourteen had been taken under Michael's wing and a close bond had formed between them.

"We're off to war," they sang, buoyed on by a cheering, flag-waving nation. The light hearts soon grew heavy. Back in the nightmare of war, the Sergeant Major's face was an ugly crimson, his eyes bulging as he stared down at two of his soldiers in an unnatural embrace.

"What the hell is this? You ran! You pair of Nancy boys ran away! I'm not having a couple of queers in my Battalion. You're under arrest. I'll get rid of you. You'll get sent away to join the rest of the bloody fairies."

The Sergeant-at-Arms was found and, amidst the noise, blood and chaos, Michael and Arthur were handcuffed and taken away to a makeshift cell.

The Court Martial was convened next day in the Officers' dug-out.

"I'm frightened," whispered Arthur. "What will they do with us?"

"'We'll be sent home, I expect," soothed Michael, knowing full well what the penalty would be.

The Sergeant Major brought Michael and Arthur to attention while three officers and two of the soldier's contemporaries marched stiffly into the cramped room.

"You are charged with running away in the face of the enemy, losing your rifles and …" the Colonel coughed, embarrassed, "performing a homosexual act. What do you have to say?"

Arthur stuttered, terrified: "You can't prosecute Michael. He saved my life by pulling me into the crater. Yes, I was scared, we're all scared but I didn't know what I was doing."

Michael was quite calm. "You can't condemn Arthur, Sir. He's only fifteen. He lied about his age to serve his country and yes, to be with me. Okay, we're more than just friends but it's not a crime in our eyes to feel the way we do."

"We cannot condone your action," said the Colonel, "otherwise everyone would run away when they were scared and, as the older of the two of you," he looked at Michael, "I hold you responsible for your disgusting feelings."

He positioned his ceremonial sword to point at Michael. Michael braced himself. Although the position of the sword was usually kept for condemned officers, Michael knew full well what it meant for him.

"You will be taken out at dawn tomorrow and shot.You," he said to Arthur, "will be sent home and never be accepted into the army again."

Michael bowed his head in resignation but Arthur cried hysterically. "No! No! Please don't take him. Please, oh God! I love you, Michael."

"I love you too, Arthur. Don't forget me."

"I won't" sobbed Arthur. "I'll never forget you."

That all happened decades ago. Arthur was now back at the cemetery where he finished cleaning the plaque he had laid for Michael but then turned to the gravestone next to it. He laid his roses and wept as he stared at the inscription.

'Rose Carter, devoted wife to Arthur and mother to Cecilia.'

"I'm glad you know about Michael now, Rosie. I wanted to tell you many times but, I was very young then and the subject was taboo. It wasn't the done thing to love a man and, although I'll never forget him, I grew up and fell in love with you." Arthur chuckled. "I wouldn't be sent away with the fairies these days. It's all become acceptable."

A cheerful voice hailed from across the cemetery: "Are you ready to go home Gramps? Apparently, there's a telegram waiting for you. I think it's from The Queen."

Genre: Non-Fiction.   Topic: "Surprise". By Alan Pearce

Girlfriends shock

It was 1963: *Top of the Pops* and long hair and Beatles-mania and all that. My school and university friend Frank and I still lived at home with our parents, having not yet been able to break the financial shackles that bound us to them. But this did mean that we had a little more disposable income than we would have done had we been living in digs, or a bedsit, or a shared flat. With evening and weekend work, I had even managed to buy a small 'banger' – an A35 van – grey, as they all were, with only two seats but a very useful cargo space behind the two front seats. Just big enough to hold a mattress.

We were both very sociable, gregarious even. And we partied and raved whenever we could after the necessary long hours of study had been put in. The van was very useful in getting us around.

We had girlfriends in the same town. They were both very sweet. And very proper. My girlfriend was called Mary, and her mother was a nice, kind widow, and very protective of her. Frank's girlfriend was called Rosemary. Her parents were equally protective, perhaps more so. They were a good, middle-class English family – Church of England, of course – and had all the social mores (or social hang-ups, whatever) to go with it. "Proper" is certainly the best appellation; they were very "proper" indeed. I doubt that very much happened upstairs with the light on, other than in the bathroom. Whatever they had taught their daughter apart from "Don't", I cannot imagine.

One December day, Frank and I decided to ask our girlfriends out for the evening. They, and we, were looking forward to it even though we had different aspirations. We were going to go to a film. A new film. In town. Would probably sit in the back seats.

First, I collected Frank from his house. Then I picked up Mary, who had to recline in the back of the little van. Then we went to Rosemary's house. We all went in.

They were having a late tea. Frank said to Rosemary: "We're going to that film I told you about. Are you ready?" She replied in the affirmative. We started to stand up.

Rosemary's father said: "Is that all you're going to do? Why don't you go to a club afterwards and have a good screw?"

Frank's jaw dropped, and I could see that he was incapable of speech. I felt pretty much the same. What had happened? Was this a transmogrification of the parents' ideals? What was he talking about?

Rosemary's father continued: "Yes. They're all doing it. Everywhere you go. And they really enjoy screwing. We didn't do it in our day, of course, not yet invented – hah! But you go out, the four of you, and enjoy your screwing together. You could all four screw with each other. You can tell us all about it afterwards."

Rosemary's mother leaned over and gently said: "Henry, it's called 'The Twist'".

Genre: Blank verse. Topic: "Airport". By Lesley Watts

Airport

The ebb and flow
Of humanity
Of different hues and sizes
Rushes like a tsunami
Then recedes again
Like a complicated choreographed dance
Flights are called
Passengers embark
Others wait
Mixtures of attire
And emotions
Business vs casual
Colourful to sombre
Restlessness vs calm
Happy to frustrated
All vie for a moment
In this chaotic theatre
At this time
The whirlwind of activity
Needs no competition
But then...
A cacophony of sound
Assaults the ears.
Bing bong
Heralds announcements
Barely audible
Over chatter
Wailing and sobbing

Tutting and grumbling
Of tired children
And adults alike
The travel weary
But there's laughter too
As expectation and excitement intermingle
Then …
A solitary traveller
Carves a moment.
Sits cross legged
Leaning against a suitcase
Headphones on
Eyes closed
Seemingly oblivious
Calm...Still... In the eye of the storm
Carves out space
For a moment of peace.

Genre: Fiction.   Topic: "Learning".   By Barbara Shea

Education as it is

My name is Tasneem. I'm sitting here in our freezing cold house, trying to write with the remaining stub of my pencil. Since the Taliban came again, I'm no longer allowed to go to school and my mother is not allowed to work, unless of course it's for the government, and she hasn't enough education for that. It's winter here now and there's snow on the mountains near our village, but my sisters and I still have to go down to the river to collect water for the family. My younger brothers scour the lower slopes of the mountains for wood from the few remaining trees.

Life was hard before the Taliban came, but at least my sisters and I could meet our friends at school, get an education and have the hope of a career. My eldest sister Yashfa was lucky. She finished school just before the Taliban took over our part of Afghanistan. She wanted to go to Medical School in Kabul and be a doctor, but that dream has ended now, and she is promised in marriage to a man from the next village.

At first, my father supported the Taliban, thinking that they would bring a more stable government to Afghanistan, and after years of drought, famine and war he was ready to believe that their Islamic values were a good thing. Not any more though. He's become disillusioned with how they are running the country and thinks we are going backwards rather than forwards. Women, of course, have to be very guarded in their opinions.

Still, we are learning to make the best of things. We don't have much food and since female aid workers are no longer allowed in the country, it means there are fewer people to help bring in much needed supplies to our remote area. However, Yashfa is trying to teach us younger children what she learnt at school and we hope that someday we will be allowed back to school to continue our education.

...

My name is Tracy. I'm sitting here on this freezing cold park bench, writing this on my iPad.

I could be in a warm classroom doing my schoolwork, but what's the point? The teachers say that what we learn in school will help us get a job, but I don't hold with that. Learning never did my mum and dad any good and they've always managed to have what they want and bring us up on the benefits they get.

At one time, they thought that a Labour Government was a good thing and would help working class people. But they soon went off the idea, and decided that all politicians are the same and are just out for what they can get.

When we were little, my sister Maggie used to play at being a doctor and always said that was what she wanted to be when she grew up. Fat chance. That's not for the likes of us. She got pregnant at fifteen and she's got three kids now. Her husband drives the lorries abroad and isn't home much, and that's just the way she likes it.

Right. I've nearly finished my burger and then I'll be off to the precinct to meet my mates. They don't see the point of learning either. I might even pinch some make up from Boots while I'm there. I'll have to watch out for the cops though. After all, I'm still learning!

Genre: Fiction.   Topic: "Learning".   By Tony Wilson

The Master's apprentice

The sunlight streamed into the long windows of the studio; its high ceilings and plain stone walls giving the room an airy feel. Cold in the winter, but on this spring morning, the atmosphere was one of warmth and light and activity. The Master was at work on his latest commission for the Duke. The room was festooned with canvasses, some completed and set aside, some in one or other of the many processes of production, some simply bare expanses awaiting the Master's attention. All were on easels, except the freshly stretched and whitened ones that were stacked on specially made racks at the end of the studio.

The walls and to a greater extent the bare floors bore the evidence of the work undertaken in the room; bedaubed as they were with paint, paint dust and the detritus of paint manufacture. The other apprentices were busy to this end but the boy was paying close attention to the Master, proffering paint, brushes and water for the palette.

He was fourteen years old and never in his life had he been so happy; to be learning at the feet of the Master was the only ambition he'd had for as long as he could remember. His desire had finally been fulfilled when his father had agreed to the apprenticeship.

Life had not been particularly happy for the boy, the illegitimate son of a peasant girl and a respected lawyer. Unable to live with his mother, he had lived in the house of his father, stepmother and eleven half siblings, and yearned to escaped the noise and presence of his overbearing family and follow his dream of the life of an artist. Furthermore, to free his mind, absorb the knowledge of his Master and to learn all he could in the silence of the studio after the work was done, to buy books in the market and to draw forth from his own mind the images locked within. He was also taught the classics, languages and science from the learned men who frequented the Master's studio.

His apprenticeship proved successful and, after a few years, the Master invited him to help complete commissions as his flair for painting improved. The young man developed his own unique style and, with his master's approval, was able in time to accept commissions of his own. He also created designs for machines of war under commission from the Duke, and in later life when a Master himself, produced drawings of amazing anatomical accuracy.

He spent his last days far from his own city and country under the patronage of a foreign ruler.

Today we know him as simply one of the finest artists in history, a polymath, a genius. His name will resound through history.

His name was Leonardo da Vinci.

Genre: Fiction. Topic: "Regret". By Jan Mills

Oh, Dear!

Dear Mrs Smith

It is with great regret that I will be suspending your son Jamie from school, from today. His behaviours have been deteriorating to such a degree, over the past few months, that we are unable to tolerate these any longer. If you ring my secretary for an appointment, I would be happy to meet with you to discuss this.

Dear Mr Jones

I was very distressed to receive your email suspending Jamie. I am surprised that you are taking such drastic action for what I assume is a first offence. I will make an appointment to see you as soon as possible.

Dear Mrs Smith

I am sorry you think the school has been remiss in advising you of our concerns. I have previously sent three letters to you, with Jamie.

Dear Mr Jones

I apologise for my earlier assumption. I have addressed this with Jamie who has confirmed that he had been given letters, which he 'forgot' to give me.

Dear Mrs Smith

It was helpful to meet with you and I understand the difficulties you have been having with Jamie. Becoming a single parent, suddenly, can be quite challenging.

Dear Mr Jones, David
   Thank you for meeting with me again; I find these meetings so supportive!

Dear Mrs Smith, Penelope
   I am glad to be able to help you. Jamie seems to be settling in much better at present.

Dear David
   Thank you for inviting me to join the fifth-year visit to the Castle. I thoroughly enjoyed myself and hope I was a useful addition to the staff team?

Dear Penelope
   You have become a fixture in our outings and I cannot thank you enough for your time and commitment.

Dave
   What a wonderful weekend! I felt really young again. Please don't leave it too long before we go away again!

Penny, darling
   I'm so happy we have found each other; I feel like a teenager again!

Dave, my darling
   I am so glad you feel the same. When you spoke of us being together, I felt my heart would burst!

Penny, my love
   The next time we meet, I have an important question to ask you!

Oh Dave
   Yes! Yes! Yes!

Penny, my sweet
 Do you think we should talk to Jamie about us?

Dave, darling
 Yes... but I'm not sure how he'll take it.

Penny, dear
 I'm sure you are worrying unnecessarily. Let's face it – what can he do?

...

My poor, sweet Dave
 I'm so sorry. I had no idea he would behave like that! How is your head? Have you had the stitches out yet?

Dave
 Please contact me. I'm really sorry. Has your arm plaster cast been removed yet?

David
 I can't bear this silence and rejection. I'm so, so sorry. Are you able to walk without a stick now?

Dear David
 Please don't ghost me. Contact me. Please!

Dear Mrs Smith
 It is with great regret...!

Genre: Fiction. Topic: "Law". By Viv Gough

A hidden talent

I have a hidden talent which is hidden for a reason. I don't want anyone to know about it and, as far as I know, they don't. Having said that, I am good at it. It is harmless but illegal. I am a bigamist.

I used to be an unpleasant, cheating rat but I saw the light and I am now a responsible, generous cheating rat and have married all my girlfriends. I now have three wives who have provided me with eight children between them; three homes in three different towns and none of my wives know about each other. How do I do it? I tell each wife that I am a senior civil servant with a hush hush job that cannot be talked about. I spend a week with each wife before, supposedly, setting off for two weeks to all parts of the UK and the world on secret missions. I rotate the wives and I am never actually away at all.

I have three separate bank accounts with different banks in three different names. Obviously, I keep my real name for one of them so that I have a true name for the sake of the electoral role and council tax. I have bought two of the homes in my wives' names for tax purposes and have provided them with the resources to buy their own cars in their name. I am a good provider. I am careful to regularly dispose of receipts from my wallet and change the photographs before returning to each house. All my personal documents and passports are kept in a lock-up in yet another different town. I really am very clever at all this subterfuge. It can get quite tiring with having to constantly check my agenda and remind myself where I am supposed to be but there is never a dull moment.

I can hear you asking how on earth I can afford this lifestyle if I am never at work. Some might say that I am cruelly lucky but I consider myself a bringer of happiness and a soldier of good fortune who has put his wealth to good use. I am an only child with no close relatives. By means of a disastrous house fire ten years ago, I lost my parents but gained a hefty insurance pay-out and an equally large inheritance. Add to that a lucky lottery win and I will never have to do paid work again.

My children, whom I adore, are a blessing in disguise. They keep my wives busy. My wives all work, organise childcare, solve domestic problems and look out for elderly parents so they don't really have the time to wonder what I am up to. I also love each of them and each week is spent enjoying marital bliss. What is there not to be satisfied with?

Having said all that, I still have details to sort out. One day, my faculties and memory will deteriorate and I'm not clear yet how I will organise retirement but that is for the future. I am convinced that my families are happy and my life is perfect.

Today, I am travelling to my next home by National Express and decide to break my journey at a service station and have a coffee and a trip to the gift shop before continuing on the next coach. As I collect my drink and turn to find a table, I stop in my tracks and sweat trickles slowly down my back. I imagine that the grin on my face and the wave of my hand looks faintly maniacal.You see, I haven't reckoned on Sod's Law. It seems that, because of said law, my three wives have chosen to take their parents on a day out on the same day, at the same time and stop at the same service station to buy coffee and wave in unison at the man staring back at them in frozen shock.

Maybe even someone with my talents won't have them hidden for much longer.

Genre: Fiction. Topic: "Law". By Alan Pearce

Clearly Curious Court Case

'From Mike Smith, our County Court reporter, Saturday.

CLEARLY CURIOUS COUNTY COURT CASE CONTINUES

Six insurance companies, the police, the National Association of Funeral Directors, the RNIB, the RSPCA, the TUC, the AA, the Rail Accident Investigation Board and the Federation of Small Businesses are still arguing and trying to work out who was to blame and who should pay compensation to whom. Today's court proceedings were indeed curious and have not yet come to a conclusion.

Fortunately, we have the facts. At about 3pm, the signalman lowered the barrier arm of the level crossing because a train was approaching. A scrap merchant's old horse and cart easily stopped in good time and at a good distance. A Rolls Royce stopped behind the cart, perhaps a little too close. A Mini stopped behind the Rolls Royce. As they patiently waited, a motorcyclist overtook all of them and stopped in front of the horse and cart. A blind pedestrian stopped to search his pockets for his mobile phone; he wrapped his guide dog's lead around a rail while he did so. Although he did not know it, the rail was the barrier arm of the railway crossing.

The train thundered through. The signalman raised the barrier arm, taking the dog up with it. The blind man searched in vain for his dog. The motorcyclist did what all motorcyclists do – he revved his engine and then sped off. Behind him, the horse was so startled that it reared and the load of scrap started to slide off, backwards, on to the Rolls Royce's bonnet, bit by bit. The Rolls Royce driver, seeing this, reversed hard – without looking, and crashed into the Mini.

The Mini driver, having just stolen the vehicle, decided to make a run for it. He swerved onto the other side of the road and tried to traverse the level crossing. By this time, however, the Signalman had seen the suspended dog and had already started to lower the barrier again. The dog wrapped itself around the Mini's windscreen just as its leash, now slack, detached itself from the barrier and an oncoming hearse, (fortunately without a cadaver at the time), was forced to drive off the road, down the bank and into a horticulturalist's substantial greenhouse. The Mini itself skidded off the oily track and crashed through the window of the village shop, which is alongside the level crossing.

The police have charged them all with breach of the peace. The RSPCA is taking the blind man to court for negligence and cruelty. The shopkeeper is suing the Mini driver, the Rolls Royce driver is suing the scrap merchant – probably without hope – the horticulturalist is suing the funeral directors, the scrap merchant doesn't know whom to sue but wants to sue somebody, the blind man is suing the railway company, the funeral director is suing the Mini driver, the Mini driver isn't suing anybody because he is still helping the police with their enquiries, and everyone is still looking for the motorcyclist.

The case continues.'

Genre: Non-Fiction. Topic: "Memory". By Ted Mason

Memories

A pure white tablecloth ruined by place mats, silver cutlery, bowls of steaming vegetables and plates. I'm in my Aunt Eleanor's dining room sixty years ago; a long table surrounded by familiar people. My uncle sits at the head, a large man with a head and haircut shaped in the fashion of a German Colonel Blimp. He pours another glass of red wine into crystal glasses kept for special occasions. My aunt, small and thin; always active, scuttles to the table with a brown pudding, homemade a month ago.

My father laughs at something funny. He comes out of the greenhouse in a brown coat like ones worn by hardware salesmen. He carries a garden fork. My beautiful mother, with long, black hair, smiles across the table at my little sister clothed in her best party dress.

She cycles up to our gate, jumps off to open it. I watch from my bedroom window. Still no sign of Mark, my friend. He said he would come to play.

Mum pushes her bike out of sight.

Across the table sits my sister looking very smart. Her two boys sit gazing at the brandy being poured over the pudding.

She sits in my homemade go cart that I painted yellow and black. I push her far enough and hard enough for her to zoom herself down the slight incline to the garage. The garage doors. A goal to aim for with my football.

I am woken from my memories. "Can you pour some wine for everyone dear?" asks my wife. Mandy and her fiancé hold up their glasses. I watch my uncle pass the bottle round. My father struggles into his jacket pocket for some matches. From the corner of my eye, I catch a glimpse of the Christmas tree; artificial needles and neon lights. The fairy at the top is the same one!

After breakfast, father sits in a comfy chair. He smiles at us as we anticipate opening presents. My sister crawls to the nearest gift to see if it has her name on it. Mother is still in her dressing gown. She kneels by the tree. Real needles give out a sweet smell and little bulbs light the baubles with an orange glow. "Wait for Uncle Ted to light the pudding," says my sister to her little boy. Uncle lights up the brandy-soaked pudding and I can see blue flames flickering and it is passed around the table. "Everyone, make a wish before it goes out." Now it is my turn to light the pudding; homemade a month ago. Not so many around the table now.

My friend never did arrive. I waited all afternoon. I haven't seen him for many years. Where is he now? Mark peeps over an armchair and puts on that funny voice as he wiggles his fingers in a hand puppet. There is my father's brother, Uncle Fred. Such a little, quiet man. He twitches his moustache towards Aunty Hillary; nasty old witch. Thin and cold."Anyone for cream on their pudding? Oh, Aunty, would you prefer some fruit?" Mandy pulls a cracker with Zack. Oh surprise… A paper hat!

She sits astride her brand-new racing bike. Jeans and flimsy blouse despite a cold wind. My son Ben, his arm in a sling, long hair, struggles to cut a dessert spoon into his pudding.

I walk through the park. My long hair blowing in the breeze. A large silver necklace draped around my neck. I hope some girls see me… they never did!

My wife is never happier than when she is hosting a dinner party. Christmas dinner is so special for her. Why did we always have it at my aunt and uncle's house? *Pick of the Pops* on soon.

Lawrence and Jordan encourage Ben to hurry up as they are desperate to try out Jordan's new football. Mum fills up my empty glass with Coke. "Do you want some more, Jacky?" Coincidence... Jacky is doing the same for Lawrence. Dilemma. More to drink or football? Jacky's husband rises and collects a small package from under the tree. "I hope you like it," he says to my sister. It is a necklace. My mother opens a present from father. It's an emerald ring. She loves it. I look out the window, as I did all those years ago.

"Why does it never snow at Christmas? It snows in February!" Our dog leaps over the snow and disappears into a snow-covered ditch. He reappears, head only... and vanishes again. We laugh. "Coffee anyone," asks Aunty Eleanor. Beautiful, tiny red coloured cups are filled with black coffee. "Shall I get some coffee or tea for anyone? I think I know where the mugs are," says Aunty Hillary.

And my memories mingle with the present, forever entangled and jumbled as I sit grinning with alcohol at my children gathered at our Christmas table.

Genre: Fantasy. Topic: "AI". By Barbara Shea

AI

I wish I'd never bought it. I tried to return it to the shop, but it was closed. A sign on the door said "Gone Away". The "it" in question was a cleaning robot. I'd always harboured doubts about anything which used AI, mainly because I didn't fancy contact with a machine which might be more intelligent than myself. However, I live on my own in a large house, and since my cleaning lady left, I'd struggled to find someone who would meet my admittedly exacting standards. A cleaning robot seemed the ideal solution.

It was fully assembled when I brought it home and I decided that if it was going to be in my house, I should give it a name. It was clearly male, judging by its muscular shape, and so I called it Maxwell, after a cat I once owned. I have to say that the idea of having a male at my command was quite appealing.

Maxwell wasn't particularly pleasing to look at. He was silver metal with no human touches at all and, to be honest, he gave me the creeps. I couldn't fault the way he wielded the duster though, and his mopping skills were far superior to mine. He was programmed to do all household tasks, and this programme could be changed on the computer. I set him to start cleaning at 6am while I was still in bed and by the time I got up, all the cleaning had been completed. It was wonderful.

This worked well for several weeks, until one morning I got up to find the dusting hadn't been done, and Maxwell was nowhere to be seen. I finally found him lying down on the bed in one of the spare rooms, with a sullen expression on his face. How could a hunk of metal have an expression? I don't know. All I can say is that it was quite unnerving. I switched on the computer with the idea of reprogramming him but each time I tried, it came up with "Programme Malfunction". I was at a loss. Each day there was something else he omitted to do, and each day that task said "Programme Malfunction". If I didn't know better, I'd say he was deliberately shirking, but of course, that would mean giving him a personality, and I knew that wasn't possible. Still, it gave me an uneasy feeling to have him lying around, or sitting in a chair, and without the computer programme, I was powerless.

Eventually I Googled "what to do if your cleaning robot refuses to work". There were several helpful suggestions but all of these were programme related, and then I spotted one from someone who had the same model as me. She said that her robot had displayed similar symptoms and then one day she saw him walking down the drive with the cleaning robot from next door. They were holding hands.

"Well," I thought, "I'm not having a lovelorn robot lying around *my* house. If he won't work, he'll have to go."

Since I couldn't take him back to the shop, I took him to the tip instead. I felt slightly guilty, though, as he lay there on the scrapheap, with what looked like a reproachful expression on his face. I do all my own cleaning now; it's much easier!

Genre: Fiction. Topic: "Perspective". By Jan Mills

Witness value

'Sadie Sheridan, blonde, attractive and aged 23 was rescued from assault by 43-year-old businessman, James Martin, who saw the assault and intervened.

Police have been questioning five possible witnesses.

Melanie Roberts, barmaid aged 22 years:
"I'd just finished my shift at The Grumpy Goat pub. She, (Sadie), arrived about 8'ish with her mates. There were five of them. She was really dressed up, overdressed for the pub. She had a really short skirt and a tight sparkly top that didn't leave much to the imagination!"

"Did she leave alone?"

"I think so; her mates were still drinking but she left early. They had all arrived about 8.30 and were drinking cocktails with vodka chasers and they got through some! But I heard her say she wasn't feeling well. I saw a bloke leaving soon after her and I think he had been looking at her throughout the evening."

"What did he look like?"

"He was about in his 30s, jeans and a dark top – could have been a hoodie. I can't remember seeing him before he left the pub. I can't even remember what he was drinking. He was a quiet type you don't really notice or remember. She and her mates were quite loud, laughing and joking, so you noticed them. She was quite a looker – really long legs, and she knew it – kept flicking her hair."

"What happened when she left?"

"She hugged all her mates and just went. He left about five minutes later. He was quite deliberate, if you know what I mean – like he had a purpose, which is why I only noticed him then. He had his head down and didn't look at anyone. I think he had dark hair, longish. That's all I saw and I didn't think any more about it."

Adelaide Evans, local lady aged 53 years:
"I was walking Paddy, my Jack Russell, he's a rescue. He's been with me for seven years and I couldn't have a better dog; I've been so lucky…"

"Where were you when you saw Ms Sheridan?"

"We were just coming back from the Rec. And I saw a young woman start to weave her way through the playground. It wasn't warm and she was in very light clothes. She had on a short skirt and skimpy top and was tottering on high heels. It may have been the shoes, but I think she could have been intoxicated."

"Did you see a man approach her?"

"There was a man who looked as if he was following her. I wondered if they had argued and he was trying to catch her up. He grabbed her arm and she shouted, but she sounded cross, not scared. He was wearing a dark fleece top and a woolly hat; he was dark with a dark beard and I had the sense that he was Asian – he was definitely Muslim! But I didn't see any more because Paddy started pulling on his lead so we had to go. He is a rescue dog and wonderful, you know..."

Craig and Dean Williams, brothers aged 14 and 15 years:
"Tell us what you saw."

"Nuffin! We was just sitting on the swings in the play park when this bird came through the park. She was really tasty – dressed up, you know. Yeah, really short skirt and long legs – really fit! Anyway, she was wobbling on her shoes so we thought she'd had a bit to drink and dressed like that she was asking for trouble, you know."

"What about the man?"

"We didn't see nothin', we was just having a smoke – cigarettes, like. A bloke went up to her and they started talking. He was holding her arm and she sounded cross, like she knew him. He was tall and really black; looked smart, wearing some sort of suit, really cool. We didn't see nothin' really."

James Martin, businessman, 45 years
"I was walking to my car, which was parked near the Recreation Ground. I heard a woman shout. She sounded distressed, so I looked over to the park. I saw a young woman being dragged by her arm

towards the bushes. She looked quite young and obviously upset, so I shouted at the man holding her and started to walk towards them. There were a couple of young lads on the swings, smoking weed by the smell of it. I shouted to them to help me but they ran off in the opposite direction – cowards! The girl was trying to fight off her attacker and I was getting closer, still shouting, so he let go and ran off."

"What did he look like?"

"Dark clothes, hoodie, jeans and bright trainers, possibly orange. He was definitely white, I could see his wrists and hands, but not his face – his hood was down. But white and clean shaven, or some stubble, but no beard."

Genre: Poetry.   Topic: "Journey".   By Lesley Watts

A walk

Leading lines draw the eye
And feet follow
Leisurely
Through the park
Along paved paths
Under a canopy of trees
With dappled light
Creating a mosaic
Of colour, light and shade
Rippling like water
Into a clearing
Around freshly mown grass
The fragrance comforting
Beds filled with season's
Hydrangeas and buddleias

Leading to others bursting with
Salvias, geraniums and asters
Alliums, roses, lavender
And much more
All vying for space ... light ... attention
Colours coordinated
Adding to the sumptuousness
Different heights and textures
Gently swaying in the breeze
Blocking out man-made sounds
A cacophony of noise from birds
Swooping overhead and between trees
And bees on flowers
Pollinating
Collecting nectar
Wings rapidly beating
Gently buzzing
Butterflies add to the frenetic movement
An undulating vista
Cloying fragrances collide
Threatening to overwhelm the senses
A primal need to inhale and savour
As I slowly move forward
Almost reluctant to leave
This is my favourite part
Of the commute ...
Then beyond the park
Alongside the river
Under the bridge
To a multi-storey car park
Filled with metal atrocities
Of different colours, shapes and sizes
Like a mechanical garden
My journey from here
A snarl of traffic, fumes and frustration
Taking me away from work
From town
Towards suburbs

Towards home
Where cat,
Calm,
and Cabernet Sauvignon
Await.

Genre: Fiction. Topic: "Imagination". By Tony Wilson

Holly's holly tree

Every year, a few days before Christmas, Holly's gran would say to Holly's granddad: "It's time to collect some holly from the woods to decorate the house for Christmas and don't forget a small sprig to go on top of the Christmas pudding. Make sure the leaves are bright and shiny and that the berries are shiny red". So, Granddad set-off up the road and into the woods, up the steep path to where the best holly trees grew.

This year was special because Holly was coming to spend Christmas with her gran and granddad but each year there were fewer and fewer berries on the trees and so each year Granddad had to go deeper and deeper into the woods.

This year he found only one tree with good berries on it, just as Gran wanted. It was a beautiful tree but very few berries were present. He set to work clipping off what he needed to take home and had to reach up very high to get to the last few berries. He was about to snip them off when a small voice cried out: "don't take the last berry!"

A little shocked, Granddad stopped and looked down to where the voice had come from and saw a little fairy standing up to his knees in the snow. Granddad was sure he had not been there a moment before.

The fairy was dressed in clothes made of leaves; a green jacket and trousers and a green hat. He probably had green boots on too but they were hidden beneath the snow. The fairy also had a white beard and his eyes were the brightest blue colour.

Granddad listened to what the fairy had to say. He told Granddad that every year at midnight on 24th December, fairies from all over the great wood came together for a big mid-winter feast.

He added that the fairies find their way to this special tree, under which the King and Queen of the Fairies live, by the light of the magical berries that glow brightly on that one night of the year. Even one holly berry will give enough light for the fairies to find their way to the feast, even on the darkest winter night.

"So, please leave the last berries on the tree," said the little figure, "or many, many fairies will not be able to find their way here and miss the food and fun."

"Well of course I will leave the last berries on the tree," said Granddad. "I would not like to be the reason for the fairies not getting their dinner. I shall tell Gran that I could only find the berries I have already collected."

"Thank you very much," said the fairy. "It is a shame so few holly trees give berries these days and people like them so much but each year there seem to be fewer and fewer."

"Well, I must return to my home now," said Granddad. "It is cold and I must get back to Holly's gran.She will be wondering where I am and she will want to get on and decorate the house with these leaves and berries. I have my young granddaughter Holly coming to stay with me for Christmas."

"Very well," said the fairy, "but if you are in the woods on Christmas Eve at midnight, you will see the brightly glowing berries that you have left on the tree for us, lighting the way for all the fairy folk."

"Oh no," explained Granddad. "At that time, I shall be fast asleep in my bed and so will my granddaughter Holly, but perhaps when she is older, I will bring her one Christmas Eve to see the berries shine."

"Then I will look out for you and Holly, for as you know, we fairies live forever and you have the word of the King of the Fairies, that from this day forward and for evermore, this tree will be known as 'Holly's Holly Tree'."

Granddad bowed to the King of the Fairies and said goodbye. He walked a few yards and turned to wave but the King had gone and, whenever he collected holly leaves and berries at Christmas time from then onwards, he always left a few berries for the fairies to find their way in the wood.

Genre: Fiction. Topic: "Intrigue". By Carol Waterkeyn

Cheesemaking

Ellie stirred the mixture carefully.

"What do you think Mrs D, should we add more salt?"

She smiled anxiously at Mrs Dawkins who had come over from her own farm to help Ellie with her first few batches of cheese. Her father had been in total despair since Mum died. Mum had been the strong one until the cancer took her. Ellie had subsequently joined her dad at the farm to help and maybe improve his financial troubles. She'd hit on the idea of gourmet cheese for the local farmers' markets. With milk in abundance – more than they could sell – rather than wasting it, surely it was better to use it?

Mrs Dawkins showed her how to separate the curds and they added more salt. "Time for the special ingredient, I think," said Mrs Dawkins.

Ellie added the grated horseradish and then tasted the result. "Perfect," she grinned.

They formed the cheese into rounds and left it on a shelf in the newly refurbished dairy to dry out.

"Ready for a cuppa?" asked Ellie.

"I'll say," replied her friend and they ambled back to the old farmhouse. Ellie put the kettle on and produced some biscuits to go with the tea.

"It's very good of you to help out, Mrs D," thanked Ellie. "I don't know what we'd do without you."

"Nonsense, dear. Your father helped me with the harvest. It's just nice to be able to repay the favour. Er, will he be joining us?"

Ellie noticed Dora Dawkins blush. Maybe there was an ulterior motive after all. Crafty cow.

Genre: Fiction. Topic: "Date". By Alan Pearce

Social media

I have a date at the police station tomorrow. It's not my fault. I've done nothing wrong. I'm just getting old, that's all. It's to do with social media, which I don't understand.

You see, people as old as me cannot understand what social media is all about and aren't really interested. Most of us think it's about sending friendly emails. But my wife passed over last year and, at my daughter's insistence, I'm trying to make new friends. So, I did it without using social media but using the same principles, which she told me about.

Each day I walk down the street and intervene in whatever people are doing; telling these passers-by what I have eaten for breakfast, how I feel after lunch and what I did last night. I show them pictures of my plants, my car, my family, my dog, and of me digging in the garden, taking things apart in the workshop, standing in front of big statues, boiling the kettle and doing what everybody else does every day.

I also go up to people and listen to their conversations. Then I give them the "thumbs-up" and tell them that I "like them".

It works! Just like social media I've already had eight people following me. Two police officers, two homosexuals, a journalist, a mental nurse, a private investigator, and a psychiatrist.

I wonder what they are going to be asking me down at the station tomorrow?

Genre: Fiction.   Topic: "Ancient".   By Barbara Shea

Grandma's cats

The ancient gate creaked alarmingly as Becky pushed it open and made her way up the cracked path which led to her grandmother's door. The paint, once a fresh bright green, was now old and peeling. Everything's old round here, she thought, including Grandma.

She dreaded these visits. Grandma was very self-sufficient and Becky didn't actually have to do anything for her, apart from listen to her interminable stories about how things used to be, and how much better they were when she was a girl. And, worse still, she had to put up with Grandma's six revolting cats.

Still, hopefully it would all be worth it. Grandma had no other living relatives and had promised Becky the house. Although it was in poor repair, with house prices continually rising, it would fetch a good amount when sold. In the meantime, it was in Becky's best interests to keep Grandma sweet. As Becky hadn't had a job since leaving school at sixteen, and her benefits didn't stretch very far, the prospect of actually getting her hands on the house and the money from Grandma's savings was a pleasing one.

As she let herself in, one of Grandma's cats wound itself round her legs, nearly causing her to trip up. Nasty, smelly thing, she thought, as she surreptitiously gave it a kick. Just you wait. Once the house is mine, you and your friends will be the first to go. However, Grandma loved her cats, so Becky had to pretend to love them, too.

She made her way to the lounge, and sure enough, there was Grandma in her usual chair, cup of tea in hand. However, today was different. She had a visitor. Most unusual. An elderly man sat opposite her. He rose and, with old-fashioned courtesy, extended his hand to Becky.

"Ronald Grimes at your service," he croaked. "Very pleased to meet you. Ethel has told me so much about you."

Becky was astounded. Grandma never had visitors.

"What's this all about?" she snapped at the old lady. "Who's he?"

Grandma simpered. "This is Ronald," she said, rather unnecessarily. "He lives next door. We've been walking out together."

"Walking out?" Becky exploded. "How can you be walking out? You never leave the house."

"I never *used* to leave the house," Grandma replied, an acidic tone creeping into her voice. "I do now though. Since I met Ronald, things have changed.

We're going on holiday next week to Ibiza, so I'll just need you to come in and feed the cats."

Becky was lost for words – a very rare occurrence in her young life. She was furious, but didn't dare show it. To add insult to injury, one of the cats leapt on her knee and started digging its claws in. It took all her self-control not to fling it across the floor.

Three weeks passed and Grandma and Ronald still hadn't returned. Then one day, a postcard arrived at Becky's flat.

"Dear Becky," the card read. "We are so happy to tell you that Ronald and I were married by special licence just before we went on holiday. We're having a wonderful honeymoon and will see you when we get back."

Becky couldn't believe it. But what to do? If Grandma was married to Ronald, then that would make him her next of kin, and Becky could say goodbye to the house and the savings when Grandma finally shuffled off.

Another couple of weeks passed, and then one day two police officers appeared at her door. They asked if they could come in, and very gently explained that there had been a terrible accident. Both Grandma and Ronald had died instantly in a road traffic accident in Ibiza. Becky felt a twinge of sadness as she contemplated what had happened. However, this soon passed. After all, they were both old, and everyone had to go sometime. That was the way to look at it, and at last the house would be hers. She need never think about looking for a job again. Not that she ever had any intention of doing so.

After several more weeks Becky received a letter from Grandma's solicitor. Apparently, Grandma had changed her Will recently. Her heart beat faster as she read the details. Grandma had left her a special message.

"Becky," it read. "You have been a good and dutiful granddaughter and I feel you deserve something now I'm gone. It gives me much pleasure in making you custodian of all my cats for as long as they live. Once the last one has died, the house and money will pass to the local cat sanctuary. I know how much you love them and will be pleased to have them as a remembrance of me."

Becky let out a scream and punched the wall. She couldn't believe it. Of course, she could live in the house until the last cat died, but once that happened, she would be homeless. Instead of getting rid of them, it was now in her best interests to keep the wretched moggies alive! Life can be cruel sometimes.

Genre: Fiction. Topic: "Law". By Ted Mason

False prosecution?

A side door opened to reveal the entry of the prosecution and defence barristers. As they sat in their places either side of the bench the presiding judge strolled in. As he sat on his high chair the court officer spoke.

"All may sit. Judge Grimshaw presiding; appointed High Chancellor by the ruling Council. Present are the Honourable Mr Squeers prosecuting, and Mr Hargreave defending."

There was a loud knock on the door leading to the cells.

"See who seeks entry," called the judge.

The reply came: "A wretched man guilty of heinous crimes against the state your honour."

"Have him brought before me."

Now the door opened wide enough for two burly men in uniform to drag a small boy through. They pulled him to a chair beside the defence counsel.

"How does the criminal plead?"

"Not guilty your honour."

A murmur arose from the audience. The judge lowered his glasses to squint at the accused.

"What? *Not guilty*? What does this mean Mr Hargreave?"

The Defence Barrister rose. "He says he didn't do it, my Lord."

"Didn't do it? Of course he did."

"He insists he is innocent, my Lord."

"Oh well… get on with it then. Waste of time though." The judge sat back lazily as the prosecution began the opening statement.

"I intend to prove that this disgusting piece of garbage did commit, on the second of January of this year, an obscene and traitorous act upon the citizens of this country; this golden perfection of a place, this heaven on earth. Willingly and with forethought and malice, this filth desecrated the very foundations of society."

A groan spread around the court. "Hang him," someone shouted. Judge Squeers scowled at the gallery.

Mr Hargreave rose to his feet. "The defence has nothing to add my Lord." And he sat down.

"But I didn't do it!" the boy called out.

"Ha… You admit that you know what you are accused of then?" said the prosecution. "Call the first witness."

A blind man was led to the box. "Please your eminence, I am a blind man and saw nothing."

"What did you hear on that morning then?"

"Nothing Sir!"

"So, the accused had deliberately removed his shoes so as not to be heard?"

"Must have done. I heard nothing, Sir."

The Defence rose to his feet. "And where did you see or hear nothing, Sir?"

"It were down Clement Street near the market, Sir."

"Ah... so you were nowhere near the scene of the crime then?"

"Oh no, Sir but I knew it were 'im what did it, cause my mate told me in the pub."

The prosecution jumped up. "So, he was at the scene of the crime then!"

"Are there any more witnesses?" yawned the judge.

"Call the rogue's mother to the stand," called a bailiff. An elderly woman was led to the witness box. She stood shaking with fear.

"Does your boy make a habit of committing crimes against the state, Madam?"

"Oh no, Sir. He done nothing that morning. I sent him out to see his father down the market."

"So, he did nothing *that* morning, which presupposes that he does *other* things at *other* times. I bet his father's guilty too... isn't he Madam?"

"Please Sir. He did nothing."

"I have heard enough of this case. I am going to pass sentence. Are there any mitigating circumstances?"

Mr Hargreave stood up. "I beg leniency my Lord. My client is quite young."

"Well in that case I will consider the minimum sentence. Death by firing squad."

Judge Squeers prepared to don his black cloth over his dirty white wig. Suddenly the doors to the court burst open and an important and portly man stomped to the bench.

"Sidney. What are you doing here?" grinned the judge.

Silence echoed through the courtroom as the audience recognised the Nation's Premier.

"Oh, I thought I would see how my stable boy is doing."

"Er... and who would that be?" asked the judge.

"Why he is sitting next to the defence lawyer!" Judge Squeers' face turned pallid.

"Hah, Sidney... he is innocent. It was quite obvious from the moment his mother gave evidence. He will be set free immediately."

The audience clapped, Mr Hargreave grinned and the boy in the dock passed out!

"It became obvious in the course of the trial that his mother and father devised this terrible act. They were clearly the brains behind it all and I hereby direct the police to arrest them."

"Justice done. *Well* done, Lionel," the Premier beamed at Judge Squeers.

"All rise while the Judge leaves." Within minutes the court took on the emptiness and silence of a cathedral at night... A little moan came from the floor by the defendant's table.

Genre: Verse.   Topic: "Friendship". By Tony Wilson

Henry and the Lobster

There once was a boy called Henry
who loved to be down by the sea
and each day after his schoolwork
found down by the shore he would be

Looking for shells, crabs and fossils
for stones with holes in and such things
anything odd thrown on the beach
that every new daily tide brings

One day after a mighty storm

when the clouds and the rain had cleared
Henry went down to the seashore
to locate what might have appeared

There was a sad, lonely lobster
sitting on a rock and crying
the storm had tossed him on the sand
and now he was slowly drying

"I cannot get back out to sea"
the poor sorrowful lobster said
"back to all my family and friends
all crawling along the seabed

I've tried, I've tried," the lobster cried
"to swim out to sea and back home
but each time I make my way out
I'm washed back on land by the foam"

"Oh, don't be sad," said young Henry
"we'll think of something I'm sure
together we'll find the answer
after all, that's what friends are for"

So, Henry sat down, scratched his head
the lobster beside him scratched too
Henry jumped up very quickly
cried, "I know, this is what we'll do

We can make a raft and sail it
go far out to sea, just we two
then you can drop straight off the edge
it's down to the seabed for you"

Henry first got a few tree logs
he had found washed up on the beach
then got some rope from the cliff face
that was nearly out of his reach

He lashed all the logs together
while crouching right down on all fours
whilst lobster helped with the making
by cutting rope lengths with his claws

Soon they had a ready-made raft
that Henry could easily straddle
made an oar from a piece of wood
they could make use of as a paddle

So, lobster climbed on board their craft
Henry gave a heave and pushed off
soon the pair were riding the waves
and sliding along through the froth

After paddling far out to sea
and battling against all the foam
lobster cried out, "this is the place
below us right now is my home"

So, waving a claw at Henry
and shouting his thanks and farewell
lobster dropped off from the raft edge
and down in the blue sea he fell

Down and down below the surface
the happy smiling lobster sank
while Henry turned the raft around
and paddled right back to the bank

This is the end of our story
and a jolly good tale it be
of a young boy and a lobster
who one day made friends by the sea.

Genre: Fiction. Topic: "Cosmopolitan". By Jan Mills

Cosmopolitan

"Oh my God, look at that!" Two heads swivelled immediately towards the entrance of the Cosmopolitan Club as a tall young woman entered; two pairs of eyes followed her graceful entry.

"Stop looking!" hissed Annabel at her two companions.

"But you said to look," whined Clarissa.

"Well, be more discreet; you're as subtle as a brick," fumed Annabel. Clarissa looked suitably subdued.

Annabel, wife of The Honourable Anthony Pontefroy was having her usual post luncheon drinks with her friends, Harmony and Clarissa, at The Cosmopolitan Club.

"So, who is she?" asked Harmony.

Annabel, who considered herself to be the font of all knowledge and always had to be the first with information, leant forward and said in a loud stage whisper: "She is the new wife of Harry Carter. He's back working at The Embassy."

"She's very pretty," said Clarissa.

"She's very trashy," Annabel countered. "She has no class; she's just an air-headed bimbo, goes by the name of 'Leo'. I can't think what Harry was thinking getting tied up with a girl like that!"

Leo looked over at the trio a few times; she felt very uncomfortable and had heard the spiteful comments quite clearly, although she wasn't sure what she had done to deserve them.

That evening at dinner, Leo looked across the table at Harry. "They really don't like me. I don't think I'm ever going to fit in here. I'm different."

"Thank goodness for that!" Harry smiled, "I would not have fallen in love with you if you were anything like one of the 'three old cats' as they are less than affectionately known. Take no notice."

"But they are very influential around here," Leo said, "they're the key to being accepted in this community."

"Just be yourself," Harry consoled her, "you're a beautiful person inside and out – you'll make friends naturally, as you always do."

Leo smiled gratefully and lovingly at Harry. He always knew what to say to make her feel better– ever the diplomat!

Over the next few months, Leo threw herself into the ex-pat community life. She was involved in a range of charity events and social activities and, as Harry had foretold, she soon made friends and became a popular invitee to parties. This was clearly of much annoyance to the 'three cats' and Annabel, in particular.

One afternoon, Leo entered the Cosmopolitan Club and was approached by Annabel.

"Leo, darling. How lovely to see you!" Annabel was gushing and Leo's alarm antennae were waving wildly. "I wanted to make sure you had received the invitation to the Ambassador's Ball next month. It is a bit later this year, because he's been away."

Leo assured Annabel that she had received an invitation.

"I wanted to give you a bit of background to the Ball," said Annabel. "Traditionally it's a fancy dress ball. That is not made clear on the invitation, because everyone knows, and although fancy dress is not compulsory, everyone makes the effort. This year the theme is 'Pirates and Maidens'!"

"Thank you, Annabel, it's very kind of you to let me know," replied Leo warily.

The weeks flew by and there was much excited anticipation about the ball. Annabel met with her cronies and they spent a few enjoyable afternoons discussing the forthcoming humiliation of Leo Carter.

It was a beautiful evening and the embassy looked amazing. The gardens were festooned with strings of lights and it looked like a scene from a stage show. Annabel and her cronies had agreed to meet for drinks before the event. That way they would enter together and gain maximum benefit from Leo's embarrassment. They were each wearing similar satin sheaths with evening jackets; the epitome of elegance, as they thought.

As Annabel and her cohort swept into the ballroom, she felt a frisson of anxiety that grew into extreme discomfort as she realised that the room was full of pirates and maidens!

The Ambassador, Sir Charles Walsh Harrison, entered the ballroom and, after greeting some of his more important guests, made his way to the ladies.

"Annabel, how lovely to see you," he cooed, "I see you have decided not to come in fancy dress." It was made as a statement, but sounded like a rebuke.

"Good evening, Sir Charles," Annabel stuttered, "I'm afraid we didn't know the ball was to be fancy dress."

"Strange," said Sir Charles, "I had understood that the theme of 'fancy dress' had come from you! No matter. I don't know if you have met my niece, she has only been here a few months. May I present the Lady Leonora Carter Harrison."

Annabel and her friends stood dumbfounded; speechless for once. Leo went up to them and with a mischievous glint in her eye said: "Not just an air-headed bimbo, eh? I'm cosmopolitan, innit?"

**Genre:Fact-based Fiction. Topic: Cosmopolitan".
By Tony Wilson**

Slavs from Kostromo

It was the summer of 985 AD and in the village of Kostromo on the banks of the Volga River the temperature was in the mid-thirties. Ivan was fourteen and he was fishing downriver with his brother Dimitri, seventeen, and his sister Danika, fifteen. The small reed boat that they fished from hardly moved in the early afternoon stillness; the surrounding haze enclosed them in a hot cocoon. The trout were biting – they were going to feast well that night.

Suddenly Ivan's ears pricked up as he heard shouts coming from the village, carried on the warm air disturbing the tranquillity that had been just the buzzing of insects and occasional birdsong. At that moment a longboat appeared like a mirage out of the river bend. A Rus dragon boat was bearing down on them. They had no time to react before strong arms were reaching down and plucking them from their little vessel and depositing them in the deep hull of the Viking ship. Other Slavic people were on board, tethered to one another; and the three youngsters were soon tethered with them, afraid and shaking with the shock of their capture. They wondered if their parents and their village were under attack. Danika was crying, Dimitri was trying to comfort her but Ivan was staring at the second dragon boat coming up behind them. He recognised his mother and aunt being jostled to the front of the ship by burly Vikings and forced to sit down.

They all guessed what this meant: the Rus raiders wanted a human cargo to sell in ports far, far away. They had heard talk around the fires at night, and all dreaded the arrival of the Rus. Slavs were highly prized by the people of the east. The Slavs were desired for their light and clear skin, their flaxen hair and their beauty. The boys were sometimes castrated to become eunuchs, the girls would be playthings and maids. The ships rowed on, now full of crying and despairing for a life they may never know again. They journeyed for two weeks on meagre rations until they arrived at Astrakhan and took on more food before venturing into the Caspian Sea. Ivan had never seen such a vast expanse of water, he couldn't see the other side, and the ship gently rocked as the surface of the water heaved and swelled against the hull in a totally alien way to the Volga. After another few days of travelling now under sail, they arrived at the port of Baku. Here they spoke another language unlike the Rus, their skins were dark and they wore strange clothing – long robes of bright colours and felt hats.

Here the Slavs were taken ashore to the marketplace. A crowd gathered around and the Rus made them undress for the inquisitive and leering eyes of the strange folk. One by one or in lots, all of the Slavs were sold. Ivan was bought by a man in a white robe with a black beard, along with a few other boys of his age but not his brother or his sister. He only caught a brief glimpse of his mother on the other side of the market, but despite shouting she could not hear him. With tears streaming downs his cheeks he was led away. He would never see any of his family ever again.

His new master led the Slavic boys to a train of camels, weird animals with a large hump on their backs. They travelled overland for many days but were fed better this time and treated well, providing they caused no trouble. Ivan did not.

At the end of their journey, this time they approached the biggest city Ivan had ever seen. It had huge sandy walls, as high as the trees in the forest around Kostromo. In the walls were a set of two huge gates opening into the streets of the walled city, cosmopolitan Baghdad. It was truly wondrous. The people were everywhere in multicoloured robes, the men wore turbans, and the women were covered in black dresses that only let you see their eyes. The smells and noises that assaulted the senses were almost too much for Ivan to comprehend. The market stalls sold all kinds and colours of spice and cloth, monkeys, birds and small mammals in cages and shining metalwork of silver, gold and copper.

After walking for a mile past countless traders and buildings, some on several levels, Ivan and his fellows found themselves again assembled naked and on display for sale. A huge crowd had gathered, mostly men but some women as well, all with coins to buy a boy's life.

So many Slavic people were trafficked by the Vikings that their name has become synonymous with the bondage of peoples the world over. Slaves.

Genre: Fiction. Topic: "Law". By Alan Pearce

Parking difficulties

This newspaper has to report yesterday's strange cases in the Bournemouth Courts of Regina v Smith and Gerbil, and of Smith v Gerbil, and of Gerbil v Smith and again of Regina v both of them.

The facts of the cases are not in dispute. The Waitrose car park had back-to-back, or front-to-front, car parking spaces. Mr Gerbil was about to reverse his 4x4 into a space when Mr Smith came up in his Mini Coupe and slid into the space before Mr Gerbil could back into it. He could then have gone forward – the space in front of him was unoccupied – but he did not. He stayed where he was and sounded his loud, raucous "Colonel Bogey" horn. Witnesses said that he winked at Mr Gerbil and said: "You need balls to do that."

They also said that Mr Gerbil, sitting in his large Range Rover, lined it up behind the Mini, and slowly (presumably in first gear and four-wheel drive) edged forward until it came in contact with the said Mini. It then continued to push until the Mini had been moved forward into the empty parking space – into which it could have gone in the first place. Mr Gerbil was reported to have winked and said to Mr Smith: "You need lots of money to do that."

Mr Smith is reported to have called Mr Gerbil "a bastard" and Mr Gerbil is reported to have called Mr Smith "a pentadactyl, haplorhynian, simiformian hominid."

Mr Smith then struck Mr Gerbil. The police were called.

In the Magistrates' Court, Mr Gerbil was charged with deliberately causing damage and found guilty. Mr Smith was charged with common assault and found guilty.

In the County Court Mr Smith appealed on the grounds that Mr Gerbil had inflamed him beyond reason.Mr Gerbil counter-appealed on the grounds that he had not said anything that was not demonstrably true.

We now report that Counsel for Mr Smith said: "Mr Gerbil, did you not drive my client to distraction by calling him 'a pentadactyl, haplorhynian, simiformian hominid'?"

"I called him that, but I do not know why that should have driven him to distraction and assault."

Counsel for Mr Gerbil asked Mr Smith if he knew what "haplorhynian" meant. He did not. Then whether he knew what "pentadactyl" meant. He did not; he thought it was a flying dinosaur. Then "hominid". The appellant ignored it and said: "He called me a dinosaur. And a homo. I wasn't having that."

Counsel returned to the charge: "Mr Smith, if you do not know what "haplorhynian" means and you do not know what "pentadactyl" means, why did you get excited enough to strike my client?"

"He called me a monkey as well."

"Mr Smith, we are all primates. But apes. Not monkeys. Our whole species is haplorhynian by virtue of not having wet noses, as dogs do, and we are all pentadactyl by the very fact that we have five digits on our hands and feet. Similarly, simiformian and hominid. So, everything my client said about you is true. It is also true of himself, and of the rest of humankind. So why do you seek to defend your actions by saying that you were "inflamed and driven to distraction?"

"Well, I was."

"And now we come to the language that you used. You called my client 'a bastard'. What made you think he was born out of wedlock?"

"Dunno."

"So, in fact my client's description of *you* was entirely true and your description of *him* was entirely false?"

"Looks like it."

"No further questions, M'lud."

Cases proven in the favours of misters Gerbil and Smith respectively. Judge ordered that Mr Gerbil be ordered to take a safe driving course and told not be such a prat in future, and Mr Smith be ordered to take an anger management course and told not be such a prat in future. Each ordered to pay £1,250 compensation to the other, plus £1,250 each in costs to the Court. Both told to try not to be so bloody clever in future. Sine mora. Poenam. Non obstantibus quibuscumque. Et al.

Genre: Fiction. Topic: "Cosmopolitan". By Barbara Shea

Cocktails

Sandra sat alone at the bar of a Manchester hotel and gazed warily at the Cosmopolitan. She'd never tried one before. In fact, she'd never tried any cocktail, but this was all part of her determination to broaden her outlook on life. The barman had recommended it — a mixture of vodka, cranberry juice, Cointreau and lime juice he said, and claimed it was very popular.

Well here goes, she thought, as she downed the pink liquid. It was actually rather nice, and she ordered another. Although she felt quite conspicuous on her own at the bar, she reminded herself that this was all part of her plan to do something different each week. Despite being a naturally attractive girl, she knew she had let herself go over the last few years, and had tried to remedy this by squeezing herself into a little black dress she'd had for years and applying as much makeup as she felt she could get away with. She was quite pleased with the result and found that getting dressed up had boosted her flagging confidence. Now aged thirty-one, she'd spent the last four years caring for her sick mother, giving up her job and, in time, her friends and acquaintances. Her mother finally passed away over a year since, and at first Sandra had found the grief so overwhelming that the thought of leaving the house, looking for a job, and forming new friendships had seemed impossible. Gradually though she had come to realise that she needed to start her life again, do something different, and it was that thought which had brought her to the hotel bar.

She decided that two Cosmopolitans ought to be her limit and was just about to leave when a man sat down on the bar stool next to her. He smiled and said in a voice dripping with culture: "Good evening. May I buy you a drink? I don't like to drink alone and I could do with some company."

Before Sandra had even considered it, she found herself saying: "Yes please. I'll have a Cosmopolitan."

The man introduced himself as Robert and started chatting about how he loved Manchester city centre, and the various bars and restaurants he frequented. Sandra regarded him over the rim of her cocktail glass and decided she liked what she saw. He was perhaps a couple of years older than her, with jet black hair and a smooth tanned complexion. Smartly dressed in a designer suit, he had the air of someone who was both monied and successful. She couldn't believe her luck. After several more drinks, all of which he paid for, he told her he had a room in the hotel and asked if she would like to join him there for a nightcap. Sandra assumed this was a euphemism for an invitation to spend the night, but by this time she didn't care, and anyway, it was all part of the adventure. She was single and he was gorgeous. Why not?

He took her hand and led her down the corridor. As they walked, he stopped now and again to take her gently in his arms and kiss her. She just melted.

At the door of his room, he took out his plastic key card, leaned into her again and said softly: "Just to be clear, it's one hundred pounds for two hours and four hundred for the whole night. I prefer cash, but a credit card will do. I hope that's alright?"

Sandra was horrified and sobered up very quickly. "No, it isn't," she said furiously. "Goodnight!"

As she stumbled down the corridor and out into the night, she found herself reflecting that perhaps this wasn't the best way to start her new life after all. "Perhaps I'll try the Knit and Natter group next week," she thought grimly.

Genre: Fiction. Topic: "Date". By Carol Waterkeyn

The missing keys

Minnie was feeling flustered. She was meant to be going to her doctor's appointment and, she was going to be late. As a last resort, she opened the dresser drawer to look for her absent door keys, when she found the photograph instead.

Taking it out, she smiled. It was a black and white image of her aged seventeen, with Harold, on the promenade in Weymouth on their date. A photographer had stopped them and offered to take a photo. She looked so young, so vibrant, and so confident with her long dark curls, her pouty mouth and her arm through Harold's. Harold was looking smart in his army uniform. The year was 1940 and he had just enlisted. They were so full of hope then, so sure that the war would be over soon and they could get married.

Minnie's mind had drifted off. She looked back at the photograph. She remembered making that dress – green with yellow flowers from some cotton curtain material. It had taken her weeks to make. But it had suited her, fitted like a glove and Harold had admired the way it had shown off her tiny waist. Now she looked down at her drab brown cardigan and checked skirt, at her sensible shoes and her swollen ankles.

They'd had sixty happy years, she and Harold, before he'd passed. She kissed his image on the photo before putting it back in the drawer and resuming her search for the missing keys.

It may have been a trick of the light, but she thought she saw a shadow on the wall in front of her; a man-shaped shadow. She turned. There was nobody behind her but had Harold somehow come to see her?

She would never know but it comforted her all the same.

And then she saw them. The keys were sticking out of the fruit bowl on the kitchen table. She must have dropped them there when she had been unpacking her shopping yesterday. She whispered, "Thanks Harold," before grabbing them and hurrying out for her appointment.

Genre: Fiction. Topic: "Date". By Tony Wilson

Richard and the mature lady

It wasn't so much a date as an assignation. At the age of nineteen, Richard Herring had been working for his new boss, Jane Fuller, for barely two months. He could remember the interview vividly.

As he was ushered into Jane's office, he took a seat when bidden by a very attractive lady in her late thirties. She was smartly dressed in a formal suit, crisp, white blouse and sporting dark-rimmed glasses framed by a shock of auburn hair. The attraction seemed mutual; she had hired him on the spot, barely glancing at his brief c.v.

Now, seven weeks on, he was having dinner with Jane to discuss his progress. Richard had come straight from the office after a bit of overtime. He had combed his hair however and splashed on some extra aftershave; by contrast Jane had changed into evening wear. A sparkling black mini-dress, drop earrings and extra make-up, she looked good, very good, Richard thought. She ordered for them both as they began their second glass of Taittinger. He knew she was married because she was wearing a gold band on her wedding finger plus the giveaway of the name plate bearing the words "Mrs Jane Fuller" on her office door. She was however flirting with him as if she wasn't.

He responded to her personal questions as best he could; "Yes he still lived with his parents, no he didn't have a steady girlfriend and yes he wanted to advance in his chosen career." She skated over the fact that a Mr Fuller was in residence at home but offered that she was an orphan, had in fact been one since the age of six when she and her older sister had been adopted by different couples in different cities and had been lost to each other. Fixing Richard with a mischievous smile she said she saw a great future for Richard if he knew how to keep secrets and give her and the company unqualified loyalty. His advancement would be rapid if he played his cards right. Richard wasn't stupid, he knew what she meant and he knew, she knew, he knew what she meant. After dinner, when the mints and coffee arrived, Jane suggested they might retire to a private room to continue their meeting in private.

Richard flushed at the imminent prospect of knowing his boss a lot better and eagerly agreed. The private room turned out to be a double bedroom with en-suite and was booked for the night. Richard got home at 3.30 the following morning but was up for breakfast at the usual time, explaining to his worried mother that an after-work drink with his mates had gone on a bit longer than expected.

He was in work on time. Jane however did not emerge until after 11. She looked immaculate, and after making a few phone calls sent for Richard to join her for a meeting. He wondered, as he made his way to her office, if she would be different this morning, after the night before. Now she had him out of her system, would she feel he might be less respectful and obedient towards her, would this be his dismissal interview? All these fears melted away when he was seated opposite her and realised nothing had changed overnight. She looked radiant, more alive than before, with a sparkle in her eyes as she ordered coffee for them both.

Jane told him this was not a business meeting nor a review, just a chance to be alone together. There was a knock on the door; the secretary delivered the coffees and placed them on the desk. As she was leaving Jane instructed her that she was not to be disturbed for any reason. She summoned Richard to join her on her side of the desk and he stood, slightly embarrassed, as she began to undo his trousers. Not knowing where to look his gaze fell to a photo on Jane's desk. He said: "Jane, why do you have a photo of my Mum on your desk?"

The black and white photograph in an expensive silver frame showed two young girls, one several years older than the other. The elder of the two Richard clearly recognised from family photo albums at home. Jane stopped her activity below his waist instantly and gasped before putting a hand to her mouth in horror.

"That is my sister," she quietly stated after what seemed like an eternity. The shock of the situation and its gravitas hit them both like a steam train. Both remained silent, unable even to look each other in the eye. Richard considered the situation, adjusted his attire, walked from the room, collected his belongings, and left the building.

Genre: Non-fiction. Topic: Debate. By Anon

The Great u3a Debate, October 2023
(A serious topic debated in a friendly atmosphere)

The latest Great Debate took place in the Hub on 4th October. The motion was: "This house believes that the date for achieving Net Zero should be delayed". This was proposed by the admirable John Tolley and opposed by the impeccable Colin English. The

Chairman was the irrepressible Alan Pearce, whose gavel let everybody know exactly how fair this contest was to be. In his introduction he also made sure that everyone knew the difference between "Net Zero" and "Carbon Neutrality" – not that in the end this affected much anyway, because everyone ignored it. The omnipresent Howard Wells sat on the sidelines and refused to ask a question or make a statement, however much the Chairman poked him.

Both Proposer and Opposer were very knowledgeable, but only the Opposer had brought an exhibit with him – some really dirty Alaskan crude oil in a little plastic tub. The Floor thought this was admirable. The Proposer had neither clean, polite Alaskan oil nor other items with him, but he did have graphs and bar charts, and put forward slightly more figures.

Those of the Floor had a jolly good say as well, and showed that they, too, were capable of thinking.Lots of thinking. This was confirmed at the end of this very enjoyable debate – during which every single member of the audience had had his or her say. Quite a lot, in fact. But all in the very best of taste.

We all learned a great deal: that Armageddon isn't here but jolly well soon will be if we don't mind our "p's" and "q's". Also, that there won't be enough distributive copper power cables to get Armageddon Prevention to everybody by 2050, so it really will have to be delayed. And, that it is very cold in northern Scotland. And, that house insulation is very important.

Before the Chairman actually remembered to call for a show of hands on the motion, he called for a show of hands of those who had made their minds up before they even attended (just three) (don't believe it!), and those who had changed their minds as a result of this erudite debate. (Nil. None. Zero. Zilch.

Nobody.) It might thus have been thought that perhaps there was no reason why we should all have given up our Wednesday afternoon, except that we had all had a really good time. Quite a few chuckles, and nobody was injured or harmed in any way during the course of the afternoon.

It's recommended that all the serious-thinking members of Verwood u3a should come to the next Great Debate; the date of which will be promulgated once the word "promulgate" has been carefully checked in the dictionary to make sure it's not rude. Anybody who thinks they may have been affected by anything they have heard during this discussion is entirely free to go and see a reality counsellor. The next Verwood u3a Great Debate might be even more divisive and upsetting, in which case they should see two reality counsellors. Oh, and by the way, the motion was passed with a majority of two, with one abstention – from a sapient person who expressed what most people were perhaps thinking inwardly anyway: "My heart tells me one thing but my head tells me another".

Genre: Fiction. Topic: "Cosmopolitan". By Helen Griffith

Train of thought

I'm sitting in Southampton Parkway waiting for the train to Waterloo for my commute into London. As usual, I have been ultra-cautious and have given myself much too much contingency time, anxious to get a parking space before the usual rush of commuters.

Instead of whiling the minutes away playing some mindless game on my phone, I decide the time would be better spent thinking about my next writing assignment: "cosmopolitan". Isn't that an ice-cream?

No that's Neapolitan. Wrong politan. I google the derivation of politan. It's from the Greek word polis for city or body of people. So, Neapolitan derives from the city of Naples. You can get a Neapolitan pizza too, can't you?

What shall I have for tea tonight? Perhaps I can buy a pizza on the way home to save cooking... I Google Neapolitan pizza. Just cheese and tomatoes really. Well, I say that but it's not any old cheese and tomatoes; they must be sourced locally to Naples.So, it's a refined margarita pizza!

Pulling myself away from thoughts of food, (I've only just had my breakfast), I return to my musings.

Cosmos would indicate something found all over the world, all over the universe even. So, people from different backgrounds... but actually it's more than that. It's got an element of classy about it. I glance at the woman across the platform, who has a copy of some glossy magazine tucked under her arm. I can just see part of an advert for some over-priced perfume that would turn me into some kind of sex goddess. Haha, that's a laugh!

I gaze back to the woman. Mind you, she does look the image. She looks like she has just stepped out of the magazine. She's dressed to kill with those stiletto heels. How can she possibly wear them all day? My feet would be screaming blue murder by the time I got home. Wonder if she does it to give herself more presence in the boardroom? So, its tailored clothes, classy handbags, Jimmy Choo shoes and cigarettes in long elegant holders... Audrey Hepburn in *Breakfast at Tiffanys*. I've never seen the film but I have the images ingrained in my mind. Clever! Just shows how we are subtly influenced by the media. Is that what these Influencers are? The social media equivalent of the marketing department?

A man in a suit positions himself directly in front of me, obscuring my view of the platform edge. Of course, it's not just a suit that maketh the man, it's the way that he carries himself within the suit. Roger Moore. An image of James Bond pops into my head. One eyebrow raised, coolly seducing a woman with a vodka martini in hand…It's almost like a veneer that he wears. Is that the essence of the man or a mask that he puts on when interacting with the world?

Each of the Bonds had their own sex appeal. Sean Connery is best. Physically though, Daniel Craig has to take the prize. Those pecs! Phwoah!

Sex in the City. Now, that was another series that locked into the whole cosmopolitan thing. Wasn't that part of the appeal of the programmes? I go back to Google. Yes, there it is, and something else… the cosmopolitan cocktail was apparently almost like a fifth member of the gang. Obviously Babycham was so yesterday.

I found a recipe. Citron vodka and Cointreau. So alcoholic oranges and lemons said the bells of St Clements, watered down by freshly squeezed lime and cranberry juice. A very fruity affair. That's probably why the makers of *Sex and the City* decided to endorse it! Gosh there were some really steamy scenes in those programmes.

My reveries are interrupted by the station master announcing the imminent arrival of my train. I stand up.

Very fruity but also a bit tarty! Well one of them was…can't remember her name.

Maybe I'll buy a custard tart for pudding.

Genre: Non-fiction. Topic: "Put downs". By Alan Pearce

Put downs (A few examples...)

Pretentiousness
At Crane Valley Golf Club, a golfer waited while everyone else departed until there was only one other left.

"Would you like a lift into town in my new Rolls Royce?" he said. The other thanked him and accepted.

They hadn't gone far, in silence, when the frustrated driver said: "I expect this is the first time you've been in a Rolls Royce?"

The other thought for a moment, and then said: "In the front, yes."

Small talk
We went to a reception (formerly "cocktail party") in Catisfield, Fareham, in 1993. Most of the people there were very pleasant, but one large, tweeded, rubicund lady in our small group was holding forth long and loud about her country pursuits; hunting mostly, bit of shooting and fishing, without letting anybody else get a word in edgeways.

Finally, and mercifully, she realised she was talking too much and turned to me and said: "Do you shoot, yourself?"

I took great delight in saying: "I try very hard not to."

National stereotypes
I had been asked to play my pipes at a Burns Night dinner in Trowbridge. It was an hour in the car. I was told: "We can't leave until six."

Therefore, I had to dress in my full highland costume before we left, there not being time to change at the other end.

Next was: "I want to stop at Salisbury Waitrose on the way up." So, we did.

I was told to sit in the car, and not come in. I did sit for a while, got fed up, and went in to the newsagent section of Waitrose right by the door. Seeing a picture of Nigella, I picked up the book. And started thumbing through.

Before long an assistant came up and said: "May I help you?"

The Fairy of the Funny Quip inside me took charge and compelled me to say, in an over-broad Scottish accent: "No, thank Ye. I'm just memorising this recipe so I dinnae have tae buy the book."

Saying farewell to Jack

An early learning experience was both educative and emotional and left a great impression on me. One of our sailors died, of natural causes, at home in his married quarter in Plymouth. An old naval tradition followed.

Technically, the dead man's kit belonged to the Crown. Practically, the Crown did not want it, and so it was auctioned on board ship – and the auction proceeds given to the widow. The auction took place in the Junior Ratings' dining hall – the biggest single open space in the ship. All ranks at every level were invited. The Master at Arms was the auctioneer – chiefly so that no-one could argue.

The first item to be auctioned was the deceased sailor's cap.

What am I bid?" called the Master at Arms.

I thought: "What a waste of time, auctioning an old cap." I was put down immediately; hard, horribly, and devastatingly, but fortunately I hadn't actually said anything out loud.

"Ten pounds!" came the first shout.
"Twenty!"
"Fifty!"
"A hundred!"

It was sold to a Leading Seaman for two hundred pounds.

Then his belt went for two hundred pounds, his collar went for one hundred, his knife for one hundred and fifty and finally it was his trousers and jacket, his "best sailor suit". "What am I bid?" cried the Master at Arms.

A voice from the back said: "Five hundred pounds." It was the Captain. In deference, nobody else made a bid at all, just to let him have it, and make his contribution.

The proceeds went, as I said, to the widow. Jack had paid his last respects to a shipmate.

Genre: Embellished Non-Fiction. Topic: "Interest". By Ted Mason

Peevis smoking

This is an interesting topic. Interesting, as it has several levels of meaning. It may be in your best interest to try writing from your own personal experiences and interests, but this may be of no interest whatsoever to those not interested in writing.

I begin by explaining that I was always interested in pursuing a career in teaching, therefore it was in my best interests to work hard at school, even in those subjects that held little interest for me... such as science and football. What really interested me was literature, playing the guitar and climbing trees. Reading was not a problem but an interest in playing a guitar annoyed the hell out of my sister who had little interest in the racket I made. Climbing trees scared my mother to death, even though she admitted that she was interested in doing the same when she was a young girl.

I did become a teacher and my first job was trying to stimulate an interest in reading from my classes. It was an interesting job. One boy, Sam Peevis, even caught his jacket on fire due to his interest in flicking a lighter on and off in his pocket!

However, a teacher must be prepared to stand in for another teacher when necessary. So it was that one Thursday afternoon the headmaster asked me to teach a science lesson! Science being of no interest to me, I was pleased to see a well-prepared lesson plan and a pile of text books in the lab. Aim: create awareness of the health dangers of smoking.

Method: use of text books pages 34 to 37. Discuss the photographs of lung diseases.

Activity: in exercise books, list the dangers of smoking and create a warning poster. Ah... well... I might not be interested in science, but I have always been interested in child psychology. Following this plan would doubtless have little effect on many students in the class. A few would be horrified, some would go to sleep and some would be very interested in the photos; mangled lungs, blood and spit, dead bodies in smoke-filled rooms.

But my interests lay in another sort of interest! An interest that most teenagers have... sex?...no. It is money!

"Close your books, sit up and listen. Peevis, I think you might be interested in this so stop flicking water. How old will you be in five years' time? ...18? What would you do with a few thousand pounds? Buy a car? Lindsey... what would you buy?

"This lesson is about smoking. You already know it is no good for your health. Some of you will not be interested in that, so let's look at some money instead.

"How many cigarettes do you smoke in a week Peevis? Oh, I know about your interest in smoking. How about 20 a week? Okay, let's pretend, shall we? How much is a packet of 20, Peevis?"

"£12 Sir!" he answered; quick as a flash!

I start to write on the whiteboard. £12 a week for a year is 12 times 52= £624. Deposited in a savings account instead.

"Who knows about interest?" @3% interest ... 624 x 3/100 = £18.72 interest on £624 = £642.72. Every year £624 is added + interest: so 642+ 624 = 1266 x3/100= £37.98 interest on £1266 = £1304.

"By the time Sam gets to 18, assuming he has banked his cigarette money each week, this is the result: £4021+£624x3/100= £139 interest on banked £4160 + last £624 payment = £4784 to spend.

"So, it is in your best interests to save your cigarette money... and you may live to enjoy the profits."

There was a strange silence in the lab. This new interest in health, science and mathematics had stirred some serious thinking.

Only Peevis had the last word as the bell went, and he forced himself through the queue to get out, pushing Jennifer over as he went. Even though he was more interested in football in the playground, he now had a new interest.

"Bloody hell. What if I could get 4% interest? That Mason's bloody clever. I was interested in those photos though. They looked super gory."

My own interest at that moment was in the chocolate biscuits awaiting me in the staff room, and it was in my best interest to get there before they all vanished.

Genre: Fiction. Topic: "Interest". By Carol Waterkeyn

"When the cat's away"

There was something rather interesting going on outside Alec and Sally's office block and the pair stared out of the window to the car park below. They were witnessing some sort of argument.

Their boss, Dave, had been summoned downstairs by his wife, and Alec and Sally could see the angry expression on Charlotte's face as she gesticulated wildly at Dave then pushed him.

"Oh dear," laughed Alec, "Do you think Dave's missus has found out about his extramarital goings-on with Laura?"

"It certainly looks that way. Serves him right, too, I reckon."

Sally was agog as she watched Charlotte stride back to her car, slam the door in Dave's face and roar off out of the car park. Sally obviously couldn't hear the conversation but guessed from the body language the sort of words used between Charlotte and Dave.

Alec hissed: "Quick, look busy! He's coming back into the building."

The young pair rushed back to their desks, put their heads down and typed furiously as a very red-faced Dave came back through the office door.

Sally looked up: "You okay, Dave? You look a bit flushed."

"I'm not feeling too good as it happens, Sally. I'm going home early. You two can hold the fort for me, can't you? If anyone rings, take a message and tell them I'll call back in the morning."

"Okay, boss," nodded Alec. "Hope you feel better."

"Yes, take care," added Sally, trying not to smirk.

Dave rushed out again and the pair hurried back to the window to see him running to his car and driving off.

"Well," said Alec, as he put his feet up on the desk and got out his mobile, "it looks like we're going to have a chillin' day today. I'm just gonna' check my Instagram. Oh, and if you're making coffee, mine's two sugars if you remember."

"You cheeky bastard," laughed Sally. "Okay, but you're doing the next ones. I'm not your skivvy."

"Bet you wouldn't say that to Dave."

Sally shrugged. "I might," and laughed.

And therefore, they were expecting to have an easy day of it with their manager out of the office.

Taking little interest in what he was doing, Alec half-heartedly sent out a few online invoices to customers for their building materials, and Sally ordered some office stationery. They answered a few calls for Dave, taking messages as instructed, and at noon, even though they weren't supposed to leave the office unattended, went off together for a leisurely lunch at the pub in the High Street. That was the plan, anyway, but Sally was taken aback on entering The George to see Dave's wife Charlotte cosying up with some tall bloke at a corner table. Sally grabbed Alec by his jacket and pushed him back through the door.

"What did you do that for?" Alec grumbled.

"Shh. Charlotte's in there being extra friendly with some guy. Getting her own back, I imagine. But I didn't want her to see us."

"Oh, point taken. Where to then?"

"Let's go to MacDonald's instead."

"I was hoping for a lager," moaned Alec.

"Never mind. You can always go to the pub after work."

As they walked into the fast-food restaurant, Alec turned to Sally. "What're you having then? I can't decide."

"Mine's a cheeseburger, small fries and a Pepsi. Here's a fiver, which hopefully should cover it. I'll grab this free table."

"Okay mate. Won't be long..."

Alec tried to balance the tray as he walked back from the counter and nearly spilled the lot when whom should they see but Dave marching through the door.

"Er, hello Dave." Alec reddened.

"What are you two doing here?" Dave asked. "Who's looking after the office?"

"Er, we fancied a takeaway for our lunch. We're just going back." Sally had grabbed her meal and drink from the tray. "But we thought you were sick?" She looked directly at him, hoping to embarrass him.

"I felt a bit better so I thought I would grab something to eat, and then come back to work. I'll walk back with you."

"Oh, er," stuttered Sally, wondering if she should say something.

"We saw Charlotte, going into the pub. Perhaps you would like to join her?"

Light the touchpaper and stand back, thought Sally. There were going to be fireworks! That would buy her and Alec a little time to enjoy their lunch before heading back to the office.

Dave muttered something, abandoning his fast food and stormed back out. Alec and Sally looked at each other. Neither could stand their boss. An argument with his wife in the pub might just keep Dave off their backs for a while.

Genre: Fantasy. Topic: "Interest". By Viv Gough

End of the collection

A man in a dark suit stood laughing and kicking, kicking and laughing. The body on the ground lay with his hands over his face begging for mercy. "No more! Please no more!"

The man in the suit took a white handkerchief from his pocket, wiped his hands and then polished his shoes on the back of his trousers. He pulled a wallet from the prostrate pensioner and extracted the paper money.

"Hmm! A hundred quid; that will do for now, old man. You borrow from us; you pay up on time, plus interest."

Back at the office, the bully's boss ticked a box on the computer. "Well done, Brutus. The old boy will pay up quicker the next time for sure.

"Here's your next job. Old Mrs Perkins down by the docks at number 27. She owes us £50. Tell her it will be £100 next week and the interest will double thereafter. You got your methods, mate, so use 'em".

Brutus enjoyed his job immensely, although he hadn't been too sure of the tactics required to start with. Somehow, it didn't seem quite right to bully and frighten old folks into paying off their loans but the boss had reassured him.

"Pensioners today are as rich as Italian Mafia and always have a stash of cash under the mattress. Don't feel sorry for them, old son. They're a cunning bunch – just a burden on the tax payer. Don't waste your time worrying about them."

It did cross the bully's mind that, if they were so rich, why did they need the likes of a loan shark but he didn't dwell on that.

Soon, he stopped wondering and started to enjoy himself. He earned lots of commission and got the use of a smart suit. Next stop then, was old biddy Perkins. She had a tea towel in one hand and a walking stick in the other as she opened the door to his ring.

She smiled. "I don't know what you're selling but I ain't got no money and probably don't want it anyway."

Brutus smiled back at the bent figure with silvery hair. Her watery eyes looked nervously into steely grey ones.

"You've got it wrong, dearie. I'm here to collect, not to sell. I want the money for the loan you took out with us. We're not a charity you know."

Her smile vanished. "I ain't got it. You said I had a month."

"Wrong, Mrs, a week is what we agreed and you're overdue." Brutus pushed his way into the hallway out of sight of passers-by and almost toppled Mrs Perkins.

"Sorry, dearie, times up. £50 now or double interest next week. What's it to be?"

Brutus saw fear in her eyes and he felt the thrill of superiority. "Now, we can have a pleasant little chat and a visit to your mattress or I'll break your dentures and flush your hearing aid down the lav for good measure."

The old lady stared at the monster in front of her. Her fear disappeared. "You evil man. Well, two can play at your game."

She looked down at Brutus' shiny shoes. He followed her gaze and gasped. They were smouldering. Smoke was floating in wisps around them and little flames began to lick at the laces. He couldn't move as his feet got hotter and hotter. He looked back up at the little old lady who wasn't a little old lady anymore. She was as tall as he was and her hair and eyes were as black as night. The bent back and walking stick were gone. She wore a crimson cloak and wielded a lethal-looking trident. Two bony, pink horns appeared through her scalp and the dark cavern of her toothless mouth exuded hissing snakes.

Brutus screamed: "What the devil...?"

"You got it, dearie! I am the Devil but not in disguise anymore."

With that, she grabbed through the flames a burning and a disintegrating Brutus, scrunched him up into what looked like a large ball of charred paper, opened her front door and threw him out. A gust of wind took him far, far away. The devil's cackle turned back to a gentle chuckle. "You won't be collecting anymore interest, dearie."

Mrs Perkins clapped her hands together to get rid of the cinders, picked up her walking stick and went back inside to put the kettle on.

Genre: Non-fiction.Topic: "Earth". By Alan Pearce

"Earth"

To look at our earth and see what it's like, you could go up into space. If you cannot afford to do that you could buy either a globe or a map. A globe will give you all the geographical facts in true perspective, but unless it's enormous you won't learn a lot. So, you have to resort to a map – large scale or small scale according to your requirements. But do remember that it is a 2D representation of a 3D object and so will have to have some sort of "projection" – spherical "projected" to flat. So whichever way you do it, there will be a distortion of some sort. For practical purposes we have just about settled on Mercator's Projection. The difficulties remain.

For example, which is further East – Istanbul or Norway? For people used to Mercator Projection, the somewhat surprising answer is Norway, which in the North extends to some 30.59 degrees East whereas Istanbul is only 28.91 degrees East. This is because of the curvature of the earth.

A similar paradox is the question: "Which mountain peak is furthest from the centre of the earth?" People are inclined to say "Everest", but this is not so. The earth is not a true sphere; it is an oblate spheroid. In layman's terms, it is flattened from top to bottom, bulging in the middle. Because of this, the summit of Mount Chimborazo in Ecuador (less than 2 degrees from the equator) is more than 6,000 feet further from the centre of the earth than is the summit of Mount Everest.

When it comes to "distance above the surface of the earth", the question of measuring it is also very relevant.

I was once privileged to hear Magnus Magnussen speak after dinner. He said: "When I was up at the University of Copenhagen in the department of Neils Bohr, the physicist, one of my fellow undergraduates was borderline at the finals so they gave him a viva voce to try to prove his worth. The question was: "How would you measure the height of a skyscraper using a barometer?"

The young man sat in silence for a while.

"Come, now," said one of the professors, "if you want to graduate you must say something or you will fail."

"Okay," said the reticent student, "well, first you could take the barometer to the top of the building and drop it down to the earth. Measure the time it takes to hit the ground, and using the equation d (distance) = ½(gravity) x t(time) (squared) this will give you the distance, or in this case, height from the surface of the earth. Secondly, and more simply, you could lower the barometer on a string and add together the length of string and the length of the barometer. Thirdly, the one I think you will expect me to say, you could measure the barometric pressure at the top and at the bottom of the building and solve the equation for height. Fourthly, you could swing the barometer as a pendulum from the top and using the equation t (time of a complete swing) = Pi x square root of L (length of pendulum) divided by g (gravity) and knowing the other parameters work out L (in this case height). Fifthly, you could get a very long ladder and measure barometer lengths up the side of the building. Sixthly, having measured the length of the barometer you could stand it alongside the building and when the sun is at 45 degrees measure the length of both shadows: L1 (height of barometer) divided by S1(shadow) = L2 (height of building) divided by S2 and since you have measured three out of the four you can work out the fourth. But personally, I would just find the janitor and say to him 'I'll give you this nice new barometer if you tell me how tall this skyscraper is'."

Genre: Fiction. Topic: "Interest". By Barbara Shea

Katie and Darren

Katie said: "I'd lost interest. Not that I'd ever had much to start with. When I first met Darren, I'd only had one boyfriend and he dumped me after a couple of weeks. Darren seemed worldly and sophisticated and I tried to show an interest in his golfing hobby, because I thought that would endear me to him. It backfired badly. He thought I really *was* interested, and from then on, at the slightest opportunity, would discuss each game he played, at great length and with much detail. I felt that if I heard one more word about Birdies, Eagles and Albatrosses, I would scream. After all, he was a golfer, not a bird watcher!

After we were married, I tried to explain that I wasn't all that keen on hearing about it and considered it an unhealthy obsession, but he just took that for ignorance, and suggested that I go with him to the Golf Club. He said he would coach me and we could spend time together in the Club House. It would expand my horizons, was the way he put it. In an attempt to keep him happy I reluctantly agreed. I was hopeless. I couldn't even hit the ball, much to Darren's anger and the amusement of the other golfers. Then it started raining. We eventually made our way to the Club House, but that didn't improve matters. I was soaking wet, hair like rats' tails and make-up smeared. It was then that I met the wives of Darren's golfing friends. They were all young, attractive and, what's more, dry. Clearly, they had never been near the golf course and no doubt spent all their time in the Club House.

Sensible creatures! It was on the way home that I gave Darren the ultimatum. Golf or me. He chose golf."

Darren said: "When I first met Katie, she was very shy and unworldly. Her main interest seemed to be watching television, particularly the soaps. What she didn't know about *Emmerdale* and *Coronation Street* wasn't worth knowing. I assumed this was because she didn't have much of a social life, and once we started dating, she began to talk about other things and even showed an interest in golf. After we were married though, it was a different matter. I tried to expand her horizons by encouraging her to play golf with me, even offering to coach her and introduce her to the wives of my golfing friends. It didn't work. Her obsession with the soaps took over again.

In an attempt to keep her happy and, much against my better judgement, I took her to Salford and paid for her to do a tour of the *Coronation Street* set. I'd thought seeing it as just a programme and not real life might help. It didn't. She raved about it and talked of nothing else. Afterwards I made the mistake of taking her to a nearby pub, and found that some of the actors from the programme were drinking there. Her favourite character was propping up the bar and proved to be one of the most obnoxious people I've ever come across. Not only was he drunk but he was loud, brash and rude. In spite of this, Katie thought he was wonderful, and even when she tried to speak to him and he made fun of her, she continued to gaze at him with adoration.

It was then I decided to give her the ultimatum. The soaps or me. She chose the soaps."

The Relationship Counsellor said: "It's good that you have tried to understand each other. Perhaps you could build on the things you enjoy doing together rather than the things you don't. It's also important to give each other space and respect each other's interests."

Katie and Darren said: "After three years together, we've realised that marriage isn't just about love, it's about compromise, and we've come to an agreement. We're getting divorced!"

Genre: Fiction. Topic: "Interest". By Helen Griffith

A person of interest

I stare at the grainy image frozen on the TV screen. Where have I seen that man before? I watch the

Crimewatch footage again. An unremarkable man comes into the shop. He looks furtively around and then makes his way to the counter where he pulls a gun on the hapless shopkeeper.

Here the footage stops and an enlarged image appears so viewers can get a good look at the man. It is not so much the appearance that strikes me. He has a beanie pulled down low over his eyes and a full beard, which covers his mouth, so in essence only his nose is fully on display. No, it is the way that he walks that catches my attention. His lolloping gait reminds me of a pointer. Quite a comical walk, in fact, and rather clumsy. On top of that his torso appears quite stunted in comparison, like you see in a child's drawing where a rotund body is held up on beanstalk legs. The man is wearing loose jeans, and black biker boots and jacket; he is definitely over six foot tall but most of that is in the leg department. I'm sure I've seen someone with such disproportionate features before; it's ringing a bell…

The next morning, bleary-eyed and only half awake, I catch the tube into the city as usual. Alighting at Bank, I am thinking of my working day ahead when I see a pair of legs on the escalator in front of me. Not any old legs, long legs that don't fill the suit trousers very well. I think back to the footage I had seen last night. Small torso, long legs!

Oh my giddy aunt! It can't be! Can it? I follow the man at a distance trying to catch a look at his face. I'm sure I've seen him on my commute before. As we make our way out of the station, I look at his lolloping gait. But, hang on, this man's clean shaven. He's quite good looking actually, even though he has an unremarkable face and short back and sides. Could it be the same man? Wouldn't it be easy to grow a beard and then shave it having committed the crime? I watch him disappear into the Bank of England. Gosh I'm really not sure. Casting my doubts aside, I phone the Crimestoppers helpline with the details and then get on with my day.

Something's not right though. A banker by day and a biker by night is totally feasible; a bit like Gangsta Granny! Too late anyway, I've reported it.

I continue to have nagging doubts and that evening I go to the Bank of England website. No, it can't be! I cover my mouth with hand. There he is, Sir Timothy Wentworth, Executive Director. I've only gone and reported a respected member of the community; a man with an impeccable career and who has a knighthood due to the work he has done around drug rehabilitation and homelessness. What have I done? I've pinned the blame on one of Britain's finest! Oh my days!

I'm now obsessed with the case. I hunt the tube for "Sir Tim"; I scroll news bulletins for updates. No luck. Then a few days later, the case is mentioned briefly because the shopkeeper dies. Poor man! His poor family! This means this is now a murder investigation. At least the police will easily find Sir Tim. Mind you, finding and catching is one thing, proving is a different matter. But what if I've accused the wrong man? I wish I knew what the police are doing. Is it Sir Tim or not?

Finally, one snowy evening in late January, the 10 o'clock news announces in its headline that an arrest has been made. I immediately stop everything and wait with bated breath until the full details are covered. A bald man with a big beard and dull eyes is shown on the screen. The newsreader tells us this is thirty-eight-year-old Ben Wentworth, who has been arrested and charged with murder. He is Sir Tim's brother, and had apparently got heavily mixed up in drugs when he was a teenager. Sir Tim, unable to save his younger brother from his demons, has devoted his life to stopping others from going down the same path. Knock me down with a feather.

I did report the wrong man but then I wonder if they got onto him because I reported his angelic brother. No matter, at least I can stop this unhealthy obsession at last.

Genre: Fiction. Topic: "Discovery". By Carol Waterkeyn

Finding a hobby

It had certainly been a life-changing day. Jeff had been called into the Director's office and, after the initial shock of being made redundant, he'd reluctantly agreed to early retirement. At least the engineering company had offered him a decent pay off.

He set off for home as normal at 5pm wondering how to tell Susan the news. Back home, he took a bottle of red wine from the cupboard and poured them both a glass; something they normally only tended to have at the weekend.

"Are we celebrating something?" Susan asked with a raised eyebrow, "or have you had a trying day?"

"Kind of both." Jeff recounted the conversation with the Director and the generous lump sum they'd offered.

"You'll have to get a hobby then, or you'll go mad," she responded, sipping her wine and cooking the dinner simultaneously. "What about golf or bowls?" she called from the kitchen.

Why did everyone assume that all retired men wanted to play bowls? It made him feel ancient and he was only just sixty. A couple of people at work had already suggested that. No, he needed something more challenging than a weekly game of bowls, he decided.

A few days later, with his last workday and send-off behind him, Jeff was free. The next morning, he stayed in bed till 7am. Susan was already up and getting ready for her part-time job at the Co-op. Jeff showered and got dressed slowly, then looked in the mirror. Should he shave or not; maybe he should grow a beard? He'd have to invest in some different clothes now; retirement 'clobber' whatever that was. Suits and striped shirts were definitely too formal for a man of leisure.

After a slow breakfast, he waved Susan off to work and walked into town. He'd decided to join the library and attempt some of those classics he'd not got round to reading. There were a lot to choose from: Dickens, Hardy, Austen, the Brontes, Shakespeare, not to mention all of the poets. He picked a random selection off the shelves and added another book curiously entitled *100 Things To Do Before You Die*. He thought it might just give him some ideas for the hobby Susan had mentioned.

He then called in at the coffee shop for a cappuccino. He looked at his watch – it was only 9.30am. While in the queue, he watched some of the harassed-looking mums call in for their caffeine hit and some office types rushing in and out with their takeaway espressos and breakfasts in a bag. Sighing, he sat down, took the first book out of his rucksack and started reading.

After a few minutes, he glanced out of the window and watched the pedestrians going by. He resumed reading. The print on the book was a bit small. Maybe he needed new glasses. At least he'd get them at a discount now. Bored with the book already, Jeff noticed a local newspaper abandoned on the next table. He picked it up and flicked through, while sipping his voluminous coffee. He hadn't realised that in coffee terms, medium meant very large indeed! He read through the headlines, attempted the crossword and then, towards the back of the paper, he discovered something interesting in the small ads and a name he recognised. Finding a pen and paper in his rucksack, he jotted down a phone number then finished his coffee quickly so he could rush home to make some calls.

Jeff waited impatiently for his wife to return at 4.30pm. He was feeling rather pleased with himself. Susan looked startled to see him when she walked through the door. She'd obviously forgotten he was now retired, although Jeff could see she was bothered about something.

"What's the matter, Susie?"

"Oh, I've had all of the awkward customers on my checkout today. There are some really grumpy people about."

"Well maybe after the strain of today, what you need is a break away."

She nodded, "Yes that would be nice. Especially now you will be around more. We'll have to fix something up."

"I've already done that. Look, it's your day off tomorrow and we are going on a little trip – so you'd better pack an overnight bag. I've found something to do in my retirement and I want to show you." Jeff couldn't help chuckling to himself.

"Where are we going?"

"France."

"Did you just say France?"

"Yes, an old schoolfriend of mine is selling a quarter share in his vineyard in the Loire valley. I'm taking up winemaking; albeit on rather a grand scale. Well, you did say I should find a hobby!"

Susan laughed. "After the day I've had it sounds wonderful. And, think of all the money we'll save on buying bottles of wine for the weekend!"

Genre: Poetry. Topic: "Discovery". By Tony Wilson

The Ship

Resting in her bed beside the cool waters in the city of her berth
She faces northwards.
Passively turning her back on the frozen waters of her fame,
A century old memory.
She is home, home from the sea.
Waves that bore her south have long erased her draft
But she remembers.
She remembers the solid embrace of the Antarctic Ocean,
Cutting through ice, frozen tears streamed from her rigging,
Making her long for Scotland, to carry her children home to safety.
Yet before she could return to her city, home to Oor Wullie, the Broons and Desperate Dan, Dundee, with the smell of whale blood still in its nostrils,
She must haul cargo far and further.
From Hudson Bay to St Petersburg and a lingering sojourn in London's bustle,
Only to be ignominiously carried in the arms of another to stately retirement.
Home to glory, see her now, she is magnificent, resplendent, gleaming.
Royal Research Ship Discovery.

Genre: Fantasy.   Topic: "Discovery".   By Ted Mason

Hubs

A discovery was made which was the result of an accident, rather like the discovery of penicillin. Necessity created an urge to make use of it and inventions created a limitless source of power. With such power in the hands of the Western Alliance, the fourth world war ended and there was peace and prosperity lasting two hundred years.

This was enough time to investigate a further discovery about how energy and space interact. It resulted in inventions that enabled our world to transform itself into how we live today, in the 27th century. No roads, No railway lines, No docks.

Jacob woke to the calming words of his alarm. He sleepily slid over and put his feet to the warm floor. The home activities programme opened the blinds to allow a stream of sunlight through the picture window. He glanced at the outside world. It was snowing in Wyoming. The forest was covered with sparkling white. Birds were singing and deer grazed among the dense foliage.

After washing and hot air drying in the steam cabinet, he dressed in the transportation suit that was necessary to wear for a day away from home.

"I'm off to work now."

"Have a lovely day, Jacob. You have a date with Melissa at twenty hundred hours. Security is on and incoming transport blocked."

Jacob stepped into the anti-contamination and transport cabinet and selected Hong Kong as his destination. The early discovery of tele-transportation, once its dangers were eliminated, had developed into a global communication infrastructure. There were no cars, no planes, no trains, no lorries, ships or buses. Anything could be sent from A to B anywhere on Earth within minutes. This had not yet extended to the new moon colonies, but science fiction writers were now talking about venturing beyond our solar system by such means.

Over years of use, enormous hubs the size of huge cities developed, dedicated to a specific service. Jacob worked at the Global Medical Hub which served every person on Earth. As such it had all equipment, staff, treatment and medicines in one place: Hong Kong. Jacob worked as a porter. There was no walking involved. It was quicker to just send a patient to the right place using a cabinet and a keypad. However, Jacob still enjoyed taking patients outside. Doctors discovered that such trips aided recovery. He would often push them along the forest paths that led to the harbour, now overgrown with reeds and mudflats where wading birds gathered. There was no noise of traffic or planes, only the breeze rustling leaves and the lapping of water on the shoreline.

Strangely there was a new interest in clearing old roads of growth and bringing them back into use, with vintage vehicles. The thrill of sailing or flying had not died. Such skills were being re-discovered by enthusiasts and a few sailing boats bobbed across the water. Jacob wondered what he would like for lunch. The problem was the enormous choice. He finally opted for a Caribbean salad in Nassau.

He would have to think about where to go tonight, too. He wondered what it was like to live in a commune, hidden from the world because they rejected the use of tele-transportation. One had recently been discovered in a remote part of Brazil where the rainforests had been restored. Televised reports showed them living like savages eating meat that they had killed and crops they had grown themselves. They looked so dirty... and happy!

That evening Jacob was ready to transport out when the tele-porter chimed. He pressed "OK" and immediately he saw Melissa was ready to come over. He pressed "OK" again and waited for her to arrive.

"I have a surprise for you. I hope you haven't made arrangements because I have tickets for the Pacific Ocean restaurant!"

"What? How did you manage that? It has only just opened."

"My boss had them but his wife is ill. He gave them to me."

This was the first commercial use of a discovery that enabled travel through water. Before this it was not possible. Melissa set the controls, entered the cabinet and disappeared.

"Going out now."

"See you later, Jacob. Have a good time. Security on in one minute."

Jacob disappeared, then re-appeared in one of a row of cabinets in a restaurant completely covered with a dome of glass. The deep sea was floodlit to show tropical fish all around it. No cooking was needed here as it was transported in by order from a food processing hub. There was no shortage of food anywhere now, as that hub could send it where needed, even to the depths of an ocean.

It would not be long before moon supply vessels became redundant. That would be a first real step into the cosmos. It was an exciting time.

Genre: Fantasy.   Topic: "Discovery".   By Viv Gough

The find

There was a dreadful storm. Harry had slept through it, unconcerned and unaware of Corinne's sleepless night. Corinne got up, made coffee and took it outside to the veranda. Their little holiday chalet seemed to be unharmed by the battering. The air felt fresh and clean so she left a note for Harry and went down to the lake for a very early swim.

She lay on her back in the glassy water and stared up at the sky. This is such a magical place, she thought, almost mystical. She and Harry had chosen an almost deserted granite outcrop on Bodmin Moor, home to Dozmary pool.

Back at home, they had worrying debts, and she wasn't sure that they could carry on with their new antiques business unless the bank would give them more time to pay. Here, though, Corinne felt at peace and felt the tiredness from a sleepless night fall away. She swam strongly for a while before heading back to land.

She looked around for signs of disturbance from the storm. Little piles of pebbles had formed on the muddy scrubland surrounding the lake. A flash of blue caught her eye. A piece of glass, she wondered? She walked carefully towards it in case she cut her foot. As she got closer, she could see that it was more than a piece of glass.

An object was half in and half out of the mud and as she bent down to pick it up, she realised that it was the hilt of a sword. The hilt looked like gold and the blue in the centre she recognised as a sapphire. She gently tugged at the hilt. Whatever it was, it was heavy but it slid slowly from its hiding place to reveal a long, thick steel blade with writing on that she also recognised as the old Cornish language. Corinne was staggered at the sword's perfection and beauty. She examined it closely with her antiques hat on and thought it could be about seven hundred years old but couldn't work out why it was in such good condition, presumably having been in the water for so long. She could hardly lift it but couldn't take her eyes off it.

But a familiar voice broke her wonderment. "Corinne! There you are! What are you holding?"

She handed her find to Harry.

"Yuk, rusty old tat. Get rid of it before you need a tetanus shot."

Corinne couldn't understand what was happening. She looked at Harry's hands and they were holding a very ugly, battered object that now appeared to be a large old knife of some sort.

"I found it at the edge of the lake. The storm must have uncovered it. It wasn't like this before you arrived, Harry. It was a beautiful sword that could be worth a fortune."

Harry laughed. "I wish it was, Corinne. It will probably disintegrate if we try and clean it up. Chuck it back where it came from. Here, let me do it."

Before she knew what he was doing, Harry had thrown the "sword" back into the lake and was heading back to the chalet to make breakfast.

As Corinne looked over the lake, a mist descended, covering the surface. She gasped and rubbed her eyes as a figure rose through it from the water. Long, flowing auburn hair spread over the pale, bare shoulders of a young woman. A crown of flowers adorned her head and a jubilant-looking smile creased a rose-pink complexion. One arm reached out and stretched high. The gold hilt of the sword, its brilliant sapphire sending out shafts of shimmering light, was firmly gripped in her fist. She disappeared under the water and rose again three times more as if in a salute of thanks for getting her property back.

The wind whistled past Corinne's ear. Was it wind or did she hear a voice?

"I am Viviane! Thank you for returning Excalibur. You won't regret it."

The mist disappeared and the sun now warmed Corinne's body. She stood for a while and tried to make sense of what she believed she had seen. As she bent to pick up her towel, she spotted a hint of silver amongst the pebbles. She picked up something like an old signet ring and brushed the mud away. It had a lion and a sword on its face and, although the engraving was faint and almost smooth, she counted thirteen dragon scales and a letter "A."

"A scale for each Knight," she murmured. "It has to be Arthur's."

A ripple moved in from the middle of the lake and Corinne waved.

"Thank you."

The Lady of the Lake might have been her imagination, but she had possibly left part of a legend that was real. She didn't think that Harry would throw this discovery back.

Genre: Fiction. Topic: "Discovery". By Jan Mills

Shouldn't have done it

Jodie loved her family, she really did; but she could not help feeling like "the odd one out" sometimes. They were four siblings and she was the middle child – Harry was four years older at sixteen and her twin sisters, Isla and Ella, four years younger.

She was also different in looks – they were all fair with shades of blond and she was darker in colour. Harry always said she must be some throwback to past gypsy blood. Harry was becoming increasingly hostile towards Jodie and she didn't know why. As younger children, they had been close but when he hit his teens, he seemed often to be angry and resentful towards her. The twins were sweet but so wrapped up in each other and seemed so much younger.

Their father doted on Jodie, and Mum seemed to rely on her, more as a friend and helper than a daughter and the twins idolised her. Harry thought it had been better before Jodie had been born; he had been the only child and the first grandchild and the central focus of the wider family. Then Jodie had come along and spoiled it all.

He was five when she was born, but suddenly, that did not make sense. If he was five when she was born how come she had her first birthday when he was still five? He had never given it any thought before but now he was going to get to the bottom of it. He didn't want to ask his parents, so one day when he was alone in the house, he hunted through all the family paperwork – passports and birth certificates – and found them all except Jodie's. Intrigued now, he searched the bureau more thoroughly and found the catch that released the secret spring drawer. There was Jodie's birth certificate. Father – unknown, Mother – a completely unfamiliar name. He had discovered Jodie's secret.

She was adopted, a usurper; she had pushed him out of his rightful place like a cuckoo chick. He felt hurt and angry, betrayed by his parents – why did they have to go out and deliberately find another child – was he not enough for them? He wanted to hit out.

The next evening, he and Jodie were at home, babysitting the twins while their parents were out.

"I've got something to show you," said Harry.

"What?" Jodie asked tentatively. Harry was often playing unpleasant tricks on her.

"This!" Harry said, brandishing her birth certificate. Jodie looked at it, reading it through a few times and shaking her head as if to undo what she was seeing.

"I don't understand," she said.

"It means you are adopted. Mum and Dad are not your parents and we are not really your family!"

Jodie stood, looking dumbly at Harry. Everything fell into place – the different looks, interests and skills; her sense of "differentness".

Harry felt triumphant and superior until he looked into Jodie's eyes that were blank and empty. She said nothing, just left the room and crept upstairs. Harry did not feel as good as he had expected to; perhaps he had made a mistake. Harry was still up when his parents came home a few hours later.

His mother asked why he was still up. He looked abashed and said he had found out that Jodie was adopted. His mother sat down with him and put her arm around his shoulders.

"We should have told you," she said. "It just never seemed the right time. And then it was too late. We wanted you to have a brother or sister and not be an only child like your dad. But I had two miscarriages after you were born and we thought we could have no more children. So, we adopted Jodie who was six months old at the time."

"I told her," Harry mumbled.

"What?!" his mum cried, horrified, "What did you say to her?"

"I just told her she was adopted," Harry replied, too ashamed to admit his cruel words.

"What did she say? Where is she?" Mum asked as she rushed from the room and upstairs to Jodie's bedroom. Harry heard his Mum's cry and realised the worst had happened. Jodie had gone. Well, Harry had what he had wanted now.

Over the next few weeks Harry and his family were swept along in a blur of panic, police and press announcements. Harry made a new discovery; far from being a usurper, Jodie was the pacifier, the peacemaker. She was the glue that held the family together.

Now the glue had come unstuck. His mother had become tearful and depressed, the twins locked themselves away together and his father had become an angry bear. Harry longed to have his sister back!

Genre: Fiction. Topic: "Journey". By Alan Pearce

A deeply worrying story

"Have you heard of restorative justice?" said the prison officer to the prisoner. Colin had been convicted of the rape and murder of Katy, teenage daughter of Mr and Mrs Carter of Leicester, and was awaiting sentence.

"What?" he said.

"Under the Crime and Courts Act 2013 and the Sentencing Act 2020, it gives victims or relatives the chance to meet an offender and explain the impact of the crime. Both have to agree to meet. It could be healing for them, and will stand you in good stead when it comes to sentencing in June."

"Okay," said Colin, "If it'll help me."

The first meeting took place in the soundproofed interview room of the prison two weeks later. Present were the Carters, the prisoner and the Facilitator, who said to the Carters: "Tell us how you feel."

Mr Carter said: "We lost our first baby in childbirth. Then, by God's mercy we had a son, but we were told it was our very last chance. Our son was killed in a school minibus crash. We prayed and prayed. The good Lord heard us and we had Katy.

Fifteen years later, this man raped and killed her. How do you think we feel?"

"I'm sorry," said Colin.

"We have prayed for her soul, and we have prayed for your soul."

"Very good of you," said Colin.

The next meeting took place two weeks later. Mr Carter said: "The good Lord heard us again and drew our attention to Galatians chapter 6, verse 7 and to Exodus 21, verse 24. They explain the true nature of restorative justice. Now, will you take over, Dear? I must just stretch my legs."

Mrs Carter started to speak. Mr Carter stood up, ostentatiously stretched his legs on the spot, walked up and down a little and finally went behind the Facilitator. In a well-rehearsed movement, he leaned down and put his huge, highly muscled arm around the Facilitator's neck and dragged him backwards before he could hit the panic button under his end of the table. He squeezed very hard, and as the Facilitator gasped for breath pushed a pre-prepared wad of chloroform-soaked cloth over his mouth and nose.

"Do continue, Dear," he said.

Colin sat, riveted, unable to move, frightened by the hugely strong Mr Carter, wondering what was coming.

Mrs Carter said: "Galatians says 'As ye sow, so shall ye reap,' and Exodus says: 'An eye for an eye and a tooth for a tooth.' We are on a journey through hell because of you. So shall ye travel. My husband is a member of a very large international society. They believe in true restorative justice, not your 'kiss and make up' stuff. They are influential and very rich – how much do you think the Israelis paid in 1960 to know the precise whereabouts in South America of Adolph Eichmann?

"When you are released, Colin, they will come and get you. It will happen within twenty-four hours, whatever you do and wherever you go, it will happen. Completely untraceably. And, believe me, what they do to you will be worse than what you did to our Katy. The difference, Colin, is that they won't kill you. But you won't be able to see any more, or hear any more, or speak, or walk. And you certainly won't be capable of committing any more similar crimes."

The Facilitator was beginning to come to, and she knew that she had only a few seconds left.

"When we leave, we will be charged with assault and complicity. He will get a suspended prison sentence and I will get a fine and a caution. Worth it at the price. But *you* have a much bigger threat hanging over you."

Mr Carter took over again: "You'll probably get parole in about twenty or so years, Colin. In fact, we intend to get some kind lovey-dovey organisation to write to the court and ask them to release you as soon as you satisfy the parole regulations. For obvious reasons. If I may give you some advice, however Colin, your only possible chance is to assault a prison officer after about fifteen years, and keep on doing it, year on year. I personally hope you fail in your attempts to stay in prison, though. Because we are waiting, with our equipment. We can wait as long as it takes. For now, however, we bid you 'au revoir', 'hasta la vista', 'do svidaniye'. 'Bye for now,' Colin."

Mr Carter released the Facilitator and slapped his face to bring him round.

"Sorry about that," he said.

Genre: Fiction. Topic: "Discovery". By Barbara Shea

Hiding in the wardrobe

I was nine years old and hiding in the wardrobe. My cousin George had said it would be fun to play hide and seek, but it didn't feel like fun, crouched there amongst the musty smelling clothes and mothballs.

My parents and I were staying with my mother's sister Aunt Patricia, her husband Uncle Robert, and George for a few days. It was the first time I had seen them since the end of the war two years ago and it was all a bit awkward at first, but George and I soon became friends again, hence the game of hide and seek.

They lived in a huge rambling old house with long corridors and plenty of bedrooms to hide in and I thought the room I had chosen was perfect as it had an enormous wardrobe where I could hide. I could still see if anyone came in because the doors didn't shut properly. I was beginning to feel rather uncomfortable.

Suddenly there was a creak and I heard the bedroom door open. I froze but couldn't resist putting my eye to the crack in the wardrobe door, expecting to see a triumphant George. However, it wasn't George at all. It was my mother and Uncle Robert. They were holding hands, and my mother was giggling like a schoolgirl. She never giggled like that when she was with Father. As Uncle Robert closed the door behind them, he started kissing my mother and she leaned into him with a sigh. I may have been only nine, but I knew this behaviour was wrong, even from grown-ups.

They started whispering to each other and although I couldn't hear all that they were saying, I heard enough to make me feel embarrassed and I must have made a sound, as the wardrobe door was suddenly flung open and Uncle Robert dragged me out.

"What were you doing in there," he said through clenched teeth. "Were you spying on us?"

"Nn...no," I stammered, "I was hiding from George. We were playing hide and seek." Uncle Robert visibly relaxed and my mother put her arm round me. I could feel her shaking through her thin summer dress.

"It's alright," she said. "Robert and I just had something to discuss in private."

I must have looked a bit sceptical, and Uncle Robert took me firmly by the arm and led me across the room.

"Right young man," he said. "I don't know what you think you saw here, but it's nothing that Aunt Patricia and your father need to know about, and I'd like your word that you won't say anything to anyone."

I hesitated. I knew keeping secrets was wrong but at the same time I realised that somehow, I had the upper hand in the situation. I gave them both a worried frown.

"Well," I said, "I don't know if I'll be able to keep a secret. You know how Father has a way of worming things out of me."

Mother crossed the room and was about to speak when Uncle Robert held up his hand.

"It's really important that you don't say anything," he said, "and to show that, how does a ten-shilling note sound to you?"

I'd hardly ever seen a ten-shilling note, never mind held one in my hand, but he must have mistaken my shocked expression for reluctance, as he followed this up with "Alright. A ten-shilling note *and* a new bike!"

I couldn't believe my ears, but pretended to consider the offer. My mother looked pleadingly at me, and so in the end I agreed, and now realising the power I had, I continued with "and I want a red one!"

Uncle Robert looked a bit put out, but nodded reluctantly. I left them both in the bedroom and wandered off. The game of hide and seek no longer held any interest for me, and even when George spotted me and claimed he'd won the game, it didn't seem to matter.

I left the house the next day with my parents, and shortly afterwards I was sent to boarding school, paid for, I suspect, by Uncle Robert. I don't know what happened between my parents, but I rarely saw my father after that. I didn't mind. He was a boring, humourless fellow anyway and I suspected my mother would be better off without him. Uncle Robert always turned up to take me home for the holidays and I never saw Aunt Patricia or George again. They say everyone has their price. Mine was a red bike!

Genre: Fiction. Topic: Discovery". By Helen Griffith

Journey of self-discovery

Growing up with my elder brother Harrison wasn't easy. He was brilliant at everything. His natural charm and boyish good looks acted as a magnet. Everyone loved him and I was always in his shadow. I tried so hard to emulate him, but this was doomed to failure from the start.

By the time we were in our thirties, Harrison had a wife, children, his own home and a well-paid job. I had a good job but it was very stressful. People kept putting on me but did I push back? No, I didn't; Johnny Doormat never said "No". Added to that, I have a guilty secret: I am gay. Oh, I know it's fine these days but I can't square it with myself and so as a self-defence mechanism, I keep myself to myself.

I remember one New Year's Eve. I sat in my lounge watching the fireworks alone, feeling very dejected. Something had to change; I just didn't want to go through my life like this. The universe was obviously listening and in early March, I saw that a new yoga class was starting up. 'Yoga is for everyone" it claimed and so, with some trepidation, I decided to give it a go. If nothing else my stress levels would be reduced and I would be a bit fitter.

The first session was quite daunting but as the weeks went by, I found myself getting into the flow. I also found a new friend, Paul. I guess, as the only other male in the class it was natural that we would gravitate to each other.

At first it was just a casual comment after class but as the weeks went by, we became firm friends. In early July, Paul invited me to the World Yoga Festival. I had nothing better to do that weekend, so I said yes. I felt quite daring as I had never been to a festival or camped even. Go me! We pitched our tents and set off to the opening concert. I looked around at happy faces, people laughing, hugging each-other and dancing. The atmosphere in the big tent was intoxicating. I stood on the side-lines wanting to let go but something held me back.

The next morning, we were up at 6 o'clock and set off for classes. Paul favoured the masterclass but I decided to do a gentler yoga followed by meditation. Later that morning I decided to try a gong bath. I let the sounds of the gongs wash over me, suddenly feeling very alive and energised. At lunch, I fell into animated conversation with two ladies. This was totally unlike me. What on earth was happening? The afternoon was spent listening to the Swamis. Was this really me? Usually, I would give this a wide berth but I found myself being pulled in by their down-to-earth wisdom, realising that there was a lot more to yoga than the physical practice.

I didn't meet Paul until the late afternoon, when I found him brewing up back at the tents. We swapped stories of our day and then the conversation suddenly became sober.

"If only I could be a good person," I sighed.

"Define good," Paul laughed, "but you *are*, mate. You're wonderful; don't be so hard on yourself. We are all on a journey of self-discovery. Each one of us is perfect just the way we are; the trouble is that we don't see it."

I stared at my friend, digesting his words and decided now was the time to come clean, to take that yoke off.

"I'm gay, Paul. It's been holding me back for years. I wish…"

"Being gay doesn't define you," Paul interjected vehemently, "you've got a value and a worth deeper than the labels we live our lives by. That's your ego talking. Get past that brain of yours and start to see things from a different perspective."

"You are not shocked by my admission then?" I asked timidly.

"Good Lord, no!" laughed Paul, "I had an inkling right from the beginning but it makes no odds. When you shift that self-defence barrier your true self shines through. You, Sir, are a fine specimen of a human and if people say or think otherwise, it's their problem not yours. Don't let their judgments shape you and your life."

I thought about Paul's words as I lay in my tent that night. I'd spent my whole life trying to match up to people: to Harrison, to my colleagues, to Paul even.

Time to find out who I really was. I felt liberated – this was my time to shine.

Genre: Fiction. Topic: "Date". By Jan Mills

Expensive date

Jen was driving to "the date" and asking herself, for the hundredth time, what on earth was she doing? Like most things, it had seemed a good idea at the time. It had not really been her idea; she had been talked into it by a couple of well-meaning friends and it had seemed a good idea on the other side of three glasses of wine. Now she was driving to pick up her "date" and she felt only apprehension.

It was difficult for a woman of fifty to find suitable new male friends and she didn't want a serious relationship, but it would be nice to have some male company for the occasional evening. She wasn't bad looking, kept herself trim and was reasonably fit. Most people meet long-term friends and partners through work, but that is not easy when you are the CEO – you can't just have a casual or any personal relationship with staff and working sixty hours a week does not leave much time or inclination for dating. Anyway, where could a single woman her age go alone to meet people?

Jen realised she had arrived and looked for somewhere to park – strange, the building looked like flats in a gated community. She had submitted her profile on the professional internet site and was going out for a meal tonight with "Silver Fox"! He had sent a photo of a distinguished-looking man and said he was sixty which was the ceiling that Jen had put on the desirable age range. The only strange thing was the letter, almost like a character reference, that was attached to the email. This came from a friend who was confirming that Silver Fox was indeed sixty years old but that he had had a hard life. Jen didn't know if that was normal. This dating game was new to her as she had only been separated a few months from her psychologically abusive husband who had moved his younger secretary into the marital home.

Jen had made an effort with her appearance tonight. She entered the block of flats which was by the moment beginning to look like warden-controlled accommodation. She wondered if she was in the right place. Finding the number, she rang the bell and after some noisy shuffling an elderly man opened the door. She wasn't sure why her date had asked to be picked up from his dad's home, but maybe he was caring for him. She realised she couldn't ask for Silver Fox but she didn't need to, he identified himself – the elderly man recognised her from her photo – she did not recognise him from his! He must have been at least seventy-five!

He hurried out of the door, locked up and grabbed her arm; she didn't have time to protest and other than give him a shove and make a run for it there wasn't much she could do, anyway. And she was too polite for that. They parked in a side street and Jen helped him into the restaurant where he had made a reservation. Oh well, Jen thought, with luck if anyone sees me with him, they'll think he's my uncle and at least I'll get a good meal out of the date – the place was quite pricey.

Silver Fox ordered an expensive bottle of wine and started on it immediately. Jen could only have one small glass as she was driving. They ordered the starters and mains and settled down to talk. He was reasonable company and Jen was enjoying the food. She noticed how quickly he was getting through the wine and she was halfway through her steak when he started making strange noises. She looked up in alarm. He had finished his meal and the wine and was now pulling faces and holding his hand over his heart.

"I don't feel well," he wheezed, Jen thought that was unsurprising as he had gobbled his food and probably had indigestion.

He said he felt really unwell, didn't have his medicine with him and he would need to get home as soon as possible. He started to get up and Jen had no choice but to help him as he bustled out of the restaurant and to the car. She opened the door and he got in, saying: "sort out the bill, will you!"

When they got back to his apartment, he seemed to recover remarkably well. He rushed inside, cried "Goodnight" and shut the door.

The following week Jen checked the dating site and, sure enough, there he was seeking "a date".

Silver Fox? she thought. More like "Sly Old Dog!"

Genre: Science Fiction. Topic: "Earth". By Tony Wilson

Mining on Triton

Far from Earth, space is an impossibly large place; here in the outer reaches of the solar system there is nothing much around. Neptune is still quite large but Triton is already receding to a small dot. Everything else, even the Sun, are just pinpricks of light in a fathomless sea of inky night. I suppose that's why they call it space!

It started off as a prosaic enough mission. A mining expedition to excavate and carry Uranium-rich ore from Triton, a moon of Neptune, back to Earth for processing. There were just two humans on board – me and Judd, the mining and loading process all being done by robots. It's been argued, by many, that a human crew is irrelevant, but this is a very expensive operation; bots have been known to go rogue, to screw up, even in this day and age and anyway the insurers insisted on a human presence. Just two; any more was deemed too expensive. These missions are calculated down to the last cent. So, we go along for the ride mostly it seems. We're both highly qualified engineers in rocketry and robots, so we supervise.

We left Earth in 2086 and all being well we would return to Earth in 2122. Not a job for a family man. I said goodbye to my parents, probably for the last time, to my siblings, friends, lover. After safely leaving orbit and checking the autopilot heading, I got into my cryotube for a dreamless sleep to Triton. It's the best part of the job, the sleep. It's a 36-year contract, the salary eye-watering, the pension second to none and you sleep for most of it. When I return home, I will have aged 11 days, mostly the time spent on Triton. 11 days' work, a lifetime salary! I will then take a year's R & R before signing on for another mission.

Judd, my crewmate and technically the senior officer, was concerned that the cargo hold was not properly sealed after the bots had finished loading all the ore. The ship is nearly a quarter of a mile long and most of that is the hold. The mighty engines are situated aft and the small human area is at the front. The bots switch themselves off a little while after we go into cryostasis but will wake if the sensors show anything malfunctioning. They stow themselves between us and the cargo.

Judd went to investigate the huge hold doors. The last thing you want is raw Uranium radiating radioactive death while you sleep. Something had fouled up. I still don't know what but when he rebooted the door system the thrusters on the main engines ignited too early, some electrical shortage maybe, and the whole ship got a violent jolt. Judd was trapped in the hold door and cut in half before they finally sealed. Some of the circuits were fried. They can be repaired, but the jolt caused the cryotubes to close with a huge bang. The lids smashed down and shattered. Neither would work and thanks to the cost-cutting we had no spares. Of course, I didn't know this until later.

Once I had processed the loss of Judd, (we weren't buddies – it was our first mission together) and like I said we aren't awake for long, but he was another human being, a fellow spaceman, so it's a shock. It was only when I had run all the flight checks twice and was sure the ship was stable and the bots had done the repairs that I realised my sleep home was a goner. So now I sit in the observation deck, watching the Sun grow ever so slightly larger each day.

I have 18 years and 2 months before insertion into Earth's orbit, with 2 weeks' rations and 3 weeks' air supply. The company will get their uranium on time but me, I'm done! They'll find a mummified corpse staring with sightless eyes to a far horizon. Even if they wanted to save me or knew of my predicament, they couldn't reach me in time and anyway two spacecraft travelling towards each other at 50,000 miles an hour, well you do the maths. Now I really wish I had taken that job in robotics at Cambridge!

Genre: Non-fiction.   Topic: "Discovery".   By Alan Pearce

Discoveries

No doubt when you think of "discovery" you think of inventions or deep-wrought healings which have been of great benefit to someone, many people, or mankind. There are other kinds of discovery which have been at best useless or at worst detrimental or deadly. Then there are some in the middle.

I myself discovered an excellent way to sterilise soil before planting seeds. Sometimes, however, there are little things in soil or elsewhere which explode greatly in a microwave, which is how my wife discovered that I was doing it. I was under pun. for a while.

Lots of other people have discovered things like that. In the 1970s, Steven Pile founded the Not Terribly Good Club of Great Britain for people with pronounced ineptitude who thought they had discovered something. The second AGM was actually the first because he failed to announce the date or venue of the first. His "Shelf Portrait", however, was so good that he was thrown out, and the club folded in 1979. He commented: "Even as failures, we failed." His books survive, though.

The real pinnacle of initial discovery failure has been immortalised by the IgNobel Prize scheme; because this encompassed discoveries which were both ridiculous and led to greater things at the same time. The IgNobel motto is: "Makes you laugh, makes you think". A good example is the "Dead spider to pick up a sugar cube" experiment. They proved that while humans have both flexor muscles and extensors (as in biceps and triceps), spiders have only flexors, which is why dead spiders curl up when they die. This led to scientists at Rice University, USA, giving a puff of air into dead spiders and then releasing it when they hovered over an article to be picked up, which in turn led to improvements in microelectronics manufacture.

Marcin Janscki, Michael Gorky, Emilian Snaski, and four others produced a paper for the IgNobels called "High Dose Melphalan Conditioning Reducing Oral Mucocitis after Autologous Haematopolitic Stem Cell Transplantation", which showed unequivocally that giving ice cream to patients undergoing chemotherapy reduced harmful side effects and led to swifter recovery.

Other IgNobel experiments included a study into why newborn ducklings swim in formation, whether nostrils contain the same number of nasal hairs, the "Five second rule", which is that food dropped on the floor will not become contaminated if picked up within five seconds, and that the anopheles mosquito (carrier of malaria) is attracted to Limburger cheese and can be distracted from humans.

The hero of the IgNobels, of course, is Sir André Konstantin Geim, FRS, Hon FRSC, Hon FInstP, a Russian born Dutch-British physicist who won an IgNobel prize in 2000 for levitating a frog by magnetism and then won an actual Nobel Prize for Physics in 2010 for his research into the magnetic properties of graphene.

My own personal heroine (and I do mean heroine because unlike the BBC I can speak good English and am not cowed by this "woke" rubbish) in the field of Discovery is Marie Curie, who discovered a treatment and cure for which there was no known disease and then died of the disease because nobody knew that it was the disease which her discovery could treat and cure.

It only remains to say that your writer today (my good self) is to join the list of aspirants. I have to tell you in all modesty and humility that I have been nominated for a 2024 award for my theoretical work on wind turbines and how they slow down the rotation of the earth, which is true, and how this affects water running out of washbasins –which is also true. All infinitesimal, of course.

Discoveries, you see, positive or negative, can lead to greater things.

Genre: Fantasy. Topic: "Earth". By Ted Mason

Fantastic space

Hundreds of streaks of pure light rushed past; red as they approached, and blue as they vanished behind us.

An endless sheet of black velvet dotted with pinpoints of diamond lay ahead. Within this warm and dangerous, volatile darkness, the jewels swirl and process across a dance floor. Here they form a horse's head, there they make pillars of hot gas. Spiral shapes slowly rotate at a million miles a second.

Then, no longer at the speed of light, the streaks vanish as we approach the outer spiral arm of a galaxy full of stars.

At the very edge of one swirling mass is a yellow dot; not huge red, nor tiny blue or white. It spews plumes of power over the black, black curtain. The small dot grows, and with it her children can be seen. Nearest is a small burnt and shrivelled baby, and further away is a sickly green one. Red, yet cold, is another and further away and growing larger are giant obese offspring, regaled in beautiful rings and colours. But most beautiful of all lies a baby between the green and the red. It is a sapphire so blue that you are lost in its depths.

This gem develops smudges of colour as we draw nearer. Shades of brown and green. The blues of the sapphire itself develop into a myriad of turquoise and greens, and brilliant white splodges appear. And, all the while, the sapphire rotates and sways from side to side in a dance of its own, showing off its beauty; a rare gem in the vastness of space and time.

Sadly, a small, grey, and lifeless ugly sister clings to the hem of this beautiful princess's dress.

Closer and closer, we are drawn to this shining jewel. Within the blobs of colour are smaller shades of each colour, many contrasting with their surrounding backdrop. Here is an expanse of green crawling up to a line on a mountain where the colours turn grey and in turn merge into a white peak. Through more shades of green and brown run ribbons of turquoise, meeting the colours of the ocean. Some parts of the jewel have turned from green to wonderful shades of red and orange. Also, great expanses of brown and yellow are, in places, shaded from view by clouds of blown particles. The top and bottom of the Sapphire are covered by white patches: here pure, and there a grey brown. At the vermillion-coloured top, the black night sky is illuminated with rainbow-coloured light shows that sway and swirl.

There is volcanic activity here. Eruptions blast orange flames into the atmosphere. Clouds of hot ash fill the sky. Rivers of red treacle slowly wind into the sea, creating more clouds of steam.

Our excitement was over-whelming. After so long, we had found a planet to seed. There was so much to do. It might take billions of years to establish but it was a start. Our chemicals, cultures and bacteria would grow and evolve life from these warm seas, beginning in the warm oceans and ending with intelligent creatures with similar genetic codes to our own.

And one day we might return to witness our creation on this beautiful little planet at the edge of one small spiral galaxy, amidst a universe of a trillion galaxies.

Genre: Fiction.   Topic: "Discovery".   By Carol Waterkeyn

Striking gold

It had been a successful trip to Busy Bees Garden Centre that morning. When she got back, Mary Patterson made a sandwich and a cup of tea and took them outside, along with her new bedding plants. Mary manhandled her old deckchair and plastic table out of the shed and sat to enjoy her lunch. Back in the garden centre, she'd seen a very nice wooden patio table and two comfortable chairs. But, if she wanted some like those, then she knew she'd have to save up from her pension.

Mary sat and watched the sparrows and blue-tits enjoying her left-over crumbs on the bird table and squabbling over them. The bird table had a distinct lean, she noticed.

Mary pulled on her gardening gloves and set to work preparing her pots for the colourful orange marigolds she'd purchased. They would certainly brighten up her dull concrete patio. "All things bright and beautiful ..." hummed Mary as she worked the earth. She remembered singing the hymn at Sunday school when she was five. Well, these marigolds really were bright and beautiful. They were very cheery.

Then, just as she was removing the plants from the second tray, something fell out. It glinted on the patio. Mary bent to take a closer look. "Goodness me," Mary couldn't help exclaiming out loud. As she picked up the gold wedding ring, she wondered who might have lost it. She also considered what it might be worth if she sold it. But Mary's conscience niggled. Someone, somewhere, was probably really distraught at the loss.

Mary hurried down the road and was lucky enough to arrive at the bus stop just in time to catch a bus back to Busy Bees. There she walked up to the sales desk: "Excuse me, has anyone reported losing a ring today? I found this in my marigolds." She showed it to the sales assistant.

"I don't think so, but I'll just check." The young assistant disappeared for a few moments. She returned shaking her head. "No one has reported losing a ring, I'm afraid, and we can't really keep it here," said the assistant.

"I suppose I ought to take it to the Police Station, then," said Mary. She tucked it safely into her handbag and caught the next bus going further into town. Mary explained the circumstances of her find, and handed the ring over to the officer at the front desk, also giving her name and address. He looked at the ring and laughed. "It looks like you found some buried treasure, doesn't it?"

Autumn was on its way. It was time to put away her deckchair and table, empty the pots and seek out some winter pansies to plant instead. Mary took off to the garden centre once more and was just deciding between yellow and purple pansies when the assistant rushed up to her. "Oh, it's you Mrs Patterson! How are you?"

Mary replied: "I'm fine thank you dear. How …?" Before she could finish, the young lady dashed off. Mary thought it was a bit rude really. The young woman returned a few minutes later with an older woman in overalls, who smiled and handed her an envelope.

"We've been waiting for you to come in."

"But I don't understand …" Mary started to say. She opened the envelope. Inside was a garden voucher worth £100. "I think you've made a mistake. What's this for?"

"It's your reward," said the older lady holding up her hand. Mary wondered why the lady was waving her hand. Still confused, Mary waved back. The woman chuckled.

"No, love, I'm not waving; it's for this!" She held out her hand. On her ring finger was the wedding band that had been among the marigolds. "I must have lost it when I was potting up the seedlings in the glasshouse. I looked everywhere for it for weeks. My assistant told me that you had found a ring and taken it to the Police. And, I'm so grateful to you. That's the reason for the vouchers. You'll be able to buy as many pansies as you want, now."

"Are you sure?" Mary enquired, embarrassed at the attention. People were starting to look over.

"Yes, I'm very sure. Now come and have a cup of tea in the café and tell me how you found my wedding ring – if you have time, of course."

An hour later, Mary was driven home in the garden centre's truck, complete with her pansies, a nice new bird table, and the wooden table and chairs she had admired. How fortuitous she had bought those marigolds. She'd certainly struck gold that day!

Genre: Fiction.   Topic: "Journey".   By Barbara Shea

Jet

Christine was worried. Her young son Robbie, aged seven, had an imaginary friend called Jet – not a person, but a black dog which he talked to and pretended to stroke. It was six months since Christine's husband had died and since then, Robbie had been so withdrawn and uncommunicative that she no longer seemed able to reach him. She also thought Robbie was being bullied at school, although he had never said as much. In fact, he never said much at all these days.

She was grieving herself of course and, on some level, Robbie was also aware of that. She made a decision. They needed to get away. A short holiday perhaps. So here they were driving through the Yorkshire Dales, Christine admiring the rugged valleys and peaks, and Robbie talking quietly to Jet in the back of the car. It was all a little surreal, particularly since she had almost accepted Jet now as part of their little family. What on earth did that say about her state of mind?

They crested a hill, and saw below a small cottage, with smoke rising from the chimney. As they drove nearer, she realised it was a café and decided it would break the journey if they stopped and had a drink. Parking nearby, she and Robbie made their way towards the cottage. Robbie looked up at the roof and suddenly shouted: "Look, there's Jet!"

Christine, startled by her son's sudden and unusual outburst, looked up at the roof and saw a black metal dog on top of a weather vane. Without offering a reply she took Robbie by the hand and led him into the café. The interior was like nothing she had ever seen before. There were crystals of all kinds dangling from the ceiling and various ornaments of fairies and elves dotted about. There was a strange smell in the air, probably joss sticks, she thought, and she could hear the sound of harp music. A curtain with bells attached hung over a door and this was pulled aside by an unusual looking lady. Her black wavy hair hung down to her waist. Her eyebrows were pierced in several places and around her throat and along her arms, she wore a wide variety of necklaces and bangles. She was dressed in a red velvet jacket and long skirt, which swished along the stone floor as she made her way over to them. Robbie was entranced.The woman didn't even glance at Christine, but went straight to Robbie and said: "What would you like, my boy?"

Robbie, in the strongest and clearest voice Christine had heard for a long time replied: "I'll have lemonade please, and a biscuit and water for Jet."

Trying to assert some authority, Christine joined in with: "And I'll have a cup of tea please."

The woman disappeared and Christine gazed at her son. He, in turn, was staring at a picture on the wall. "Look Mum," he said, "it's a picture of Jet."

Christine looked towards the wall. The painting of a black Labrador gazed back at them, its eyes soft and glowing. At this moment, the woman returned with their drinks.

Again, she addressed Robbie. "I can see you're sad, my little man," she said softly. "I can also see that Jet has helped you during your time of trouble."

Christine rose from her seat, but the woman waved her back down.

"I've had sadness in my life too," she said. "I lost someone I loved and didn't know how I could carry on. Then one day I opened the door and saw Jet standing there. I don't know where he came from, but he stayed with me for three years and his companionship helped me over the worst. Then, one day, he disappeared as quickly as he'd come. I wasn't sad though as I knew he'd gone to help someone in greater need. So don't worry if one day Jet leaves you. Be glad he's gone to help someone else."

With that, the woman left the room. By this time, Christine felt thoroughly uncomfortable, but glancing at Robbie she saw that something in him had changed. His face was more relaxed than it had been for a long time, and a small smile played around his lips. She rose abruptly, took Robbie by the hand and left, leaving money on the table.

As they continued their journey, she gradually realised that Robbie was actually speaking to her rather than Jet. Perhaps the strange woman's story had in some way helped him come to terms with his loss. She breathed a sigh of relief. It didn't matter how it had happened. She knew they both still had a long emotional journey ahead but at last she felt she had her son back.

Genre: Fact-basedfiction. Topic: "Journey". By Carol Waterkeyn

A Blackpool day out

Laurence found himself shoved into the corner of the railway carriage. He'd intended to sketch some of the scenes on the journey from Salford to Blackpool to use in later paintings, but this was curtailed when a large woman in a mustard-coloured raincoat bustled in, towing her brood of four noisy children. Accompanying her was a skinny man in a crumpled brown suit, followed by trail of men, women and children, all apparently on their annual works day out. The peaceful ambience that Laurence had first enjoyed was gone, and had been replaced by the incessant chatter of the children as they found seats, and grew more and more excited about the funfair they were going to on Blackpool pleasure beach.

The woman in the mustard coat laughed coarsely at something her husband said, then handed around barley sugars to the gaggle. She offered one to Laurence, which he took, not wishing to offend. He quietly thanked the woman, and turned back to look through the window.

"That's alright, pet. You're not one of us lot on the factory outing, are you? Sorry if we're disturbing you."

"No, it's fine," he said shyly.

"Do I know you from somewhere?" Her husband had joined in the conversation.

"I don't think so, Sir," said Laurence, hoping the man wouldn't recognise him as the rent collector who called round once a week. His face reddened and he quickly looked back though the second-class carriage window, hoping the conversation would be curtailed.

"Fairenough. You must look like someone else, maybe from the pub..."

The man looked confused, so Laurence took the opportunity to excusehimself, grabbing his artist's pad and pencils, and muttering something about going in search of the dining car, where he remained, sipping a half of ale until the steam train reached Blackpool. As the train finally slowed to a halt, Laurence retrieved his push-bike from the goods van, and descended amid the acrid steam and smoke from the engine.

He wheeled his bicycle along the platform, avoiding the noisy throng of factory workers, handed over his ticket at the barrier to be punched, and then swiftly cycled to the seafront. After some distance, he rested his bike against the low wall where he was now sitting, taking in the salty, seaweed-infused air as he opened his tin of salmon paste sandwiches and slowly ate, looking at the view before him and analysing the colours of sea and sky. He would recreate these later with Prussian blue, yellow ochre for the sand and flake white for the clouds and seagulls, he decided. He hoped his art tutor at Salford School of Art would be impressed.

He turned at the sound of the cackling voices and shouts of the workers now on their way to the funfair. In the distance he recognised the woman in the mustard coat with her family, so he quickly stowed the remains of his sandwiches back in the tin box, gathered his artists'accoutrements and clambered onto his bike once more.

About a hundred yards away, he found a good vantage point to view the fairground, and sketched the children on the carousel, the young men duelling in the bumper cars and the women on their stalls selling sweets, toffee apples and candyfloss. Laurence also drew the rollercoaster with the oval-mouthed, shocked faces of the revellers as they were conveyed up and down along the twisting tracks. Later he added Blackpool Tower to his growing collection of drawings.

Satisfied with his day's work, Laurence pedalled back to the station, and was pleased to note his previous loud companions were not on the same train. He imagined they would probably stay out late to return on an evening puffer.

Laurence's art tutor admired the painting before him. "Zees is more 'jolie' than some of your other paintings, Monsieur Lowry," said Monsieur Valette. "I like zis."

Laurence Lowry was proud of the landscape he had worked on all week. There was the Blackpool tower, here was the Prussian blue sea, and in the foreground, the funfair rides, excited children with toffee apples and lollipops, and brightly coloured balloons.

"I ee-specially like zis dark yellow accent among the crowd of brown clothing; it shows skill," Monsieur Valette had added.

"Oh, you mean the woman in the mustard coat," laughed Laurence. He had added her in for posterity. He wondered whether she would ever see and then recognise herself in one of his paintings. Maybe she would even buy one, but he doubted it.

Genre: Fact-based story. Topic: "Line in the sand".By Jan Mills

Lines in the sand

Charlie watched his six-year-old granddaughter, Daisy, playing on the beach. She was a beautiful child with an endearing air of innocence. She was happy just to amuse herself in the company of her adored grandfather. They were on holiday in a lovely part of rural Kent and the daily visits to the beach were the highlight of Daisy's holiday.

"Look Grampie, I've done my name," she cried. "I've wrote 'Daisy' in the sand."

"So you have, my darling!" replied Charlie. He looked at the marks she had made with a piece of driftwood.

Lines in the sand. As he stared at them his thoughts began to drift and dissemble. The sounds around him changed. He could no longer hear the raucous cries of the seagulls; the happy laughter of children; the gentle lap of water as the waves rolled onto the shore. He was assaulted by a cacophony of sound: loud explosions as bombs hit the beach, machine gunfire, the loud drone of aircraft, and through it all the shouts, screams and piteous cries of men in pain, in agony. Lines in the sand. Endless lines of exhausted men queuing for their place in Hell. Lines stretching back to the dunes and beyond. Lines and lines across the beach as far as the eye could see. Lines snaking down to the shore and into the sea. Lines of wretched humanity; many little more than boys. The sounds were bad enough but the smells and the sights an abomination. The stench of cordite, smoke, blood and searing flesh, an overwhelming smell of fear and panic. And the awful sight of men bloodied, blinded, burnt, broken.

It had seemed there was no hope for the thousands of troops cut off by the sea from further escape from their enemy. It had seemed they were all going to die. And yet their rescuers came from the sea. Vessels of every description arrived in their hundreds: warships, steamers, merchant ships, lifeboats, pleasure craft, fishing boats, yachts. Many of their rescuers were civilians – people who were risking their lives to make the trip into a war zone to save the lives of the stranded troops. The sheer bravery and selflessness of these ordinary people shone like a beacon of hope in the darkness of the troops' despair.

Charlie could remember every detail of his rescue. He had reached the front of one of the lines on the fifth day of the rescue operation. He had been standing waist deep in the sea for several hours and was then helped onto a small boat that ferried them to a fishing trawler to start the journey across the Channel. It had felt as though he had been plucked from the pits of Hell. Soaked from the waist with heavy sodden uniform; cold and hungry, he had been comforted by the wonderful men who had saved him and his mates and given them a ride home. They were some of the lucky ones!

Operation Dynamo ran from 27th May to 4th June 1940. 338,226 Allied troops were rescued from Dunkirk in over 861 vessels. Of the Britons left behind 11,000 died and 40,000 were captured and imprisoned.

Charlie looked at Daisy playing in the sand. Her sweet face looked up at him, her eyes sparkling with open love, joy and mischief. Had it all been worth it? Hell, yes!

Genre: Fiction. Topic: "Line in the sand". By Helen Griffith

A line in the sand

A weekend in Barmouth, away from the pressures of work and the demands of his mother living next door, was just what we needed for some "us" time. The weather was wonderful. We spent the first day hiking the panorama walk, looking out over the estuary towards the railway and Fairbourne.

After a delicious evening meal, we walked along the beach towards the town, watching the sinking sun dancing on the waves. Both of us were lost in our thoughts, neither willing to open the conversation that needed to be had.

As we made our way along the beach, Rob picked up a stick and carved our names in the damp sand surrounded by a heart. Was this what I wanted? I recalled that the heart of us was once full of life, full of energy. We were young and enthusiastic for life's adventures. Five years down the line and that heart was depleted, starved of oxygen.

I suddenly knew what I had to do. If I'm honest I'd known all along but hadn't had the courage to take the initiative. Gently, I took the stick from Rob and drew a line in the sand: though the heart, through us, through our marriage. I turned to Rob, His jaw had dropped and he stood stunned by my actions.

"What are you doing?" He stammered.

"I can't do this anymore. I'm sorry Rob, I'm leaving you."

For a moment I watched as a range of emotions passed across his face as he decided which was the best fit for the situation. In the end he settled for the wronged husband look.

"I know things haven't been too good between us but we can fix that can't we?" he pleaded.

"Maybe we could have once, but not now I know about Monica. How could you, Rob?"

I turned and ran back up the beach leaving him open-mouthed, knowing the game was up. I sat on a nearby wall watching the sun set. I yearned to go back and undo the last five minutes as I knew I still loved him very much but pride and self-preservation stopped me from doing so. It was all very well turning a blind eye to his other flings but my own sister was a steptoo far!

Genre: Fantasy. Topic: "Journey". By Viv Gough

Dolls and things

Angelina doll waited until she could hear Chloe's steady breathing before she opened one eye. She moved her head slowly, looked around the bedroom and opened the other eye. She nudged New Lucy Doll.

"Wake up. Chloe's asleep and it's time to party."

"What do you mean? Aren't we supposed to sleep?"

"We can sleep while Chloe is at school tomorrow."

"Where's the party then? It seems very quiet and dark to me."

"We're going over the garden wall, Lucy. That's where it all happens. C'mon, let your hair down." Angelina tied two of Chloe's skipping ropes together and tied one end to the chair leg. She threw the other end out of the window and climbed down.

"I don't like heights," whispered Lucy.

"Don't be such a wimp. You're a doll. What's the worst that can happen if you fall? Your legs or arms will come off. Don't worry, Chloe's dad is a dab hand at putting them back on. They might look a bit odd but you'll survive."

The dolls reached the garden wall where Angelina put two fingers in her mouth and whistled. A smiling black face appeared over the top, followed by eight, hairy legs.

"Hi, Incy Wincy," said Angelina. "Thanks for waiting."

Incy lowered himself to the ground, weaving a strong, shiny thread as he did so. Angelina and Lucy climbed up the thread, followed by Incy. He chuckled. "Should have put your jeans on, girls, you look very pretty from where I am."

Lucy blushed but Angelina laughed, "Don't mind him, Lucy, he's armless."

"Two things to watch out for when we get over, Lucy. Avoid the gremlins and keep your eye on the gnomes. They are full of mischief and aren't as innocent as they look."

Angelina led the way to the bottom of the garden into a tiny world of fairy-lights and strange music. Lucy looked around in amazement. There were fairies, elves, gnomes, dolls and all sorts of toys swaying to the music, laughing, shouting, seemingly oblivious to the sleeping world outside of the garden. A couple of beautiful dolls came over to Angelina. Both were smoking.

"That can't be good for them," said Lucy.

"Hi guys," said Angelina. "Lucy, these are my mates Barbie and Ken."

"Hello, Lucy. Here, have a drag. Get in the mood."

Lucy didn't really want one as she knew it was bad and she didn't like the weedy smell but she didn't want to look like a party-pooper. They giggled and strolled away, hugging each-other. A Jack-in-the-Box jumped up from behind the bar with shot glasses in his hands. "Here, the first drink is on the house. Enjoy."

After a couple more drinks, Lucy began to relax and Angelina took her over to Humpty Dumpty who seemed to be in charge of the food. He wobbled backwards and forwards.

"What do you recommend we eat?" asked Lucy.

"Try the mushrooms. They're magic! They're magic for me anyway," he smiled.

The dolls danced and sang to the Karaoke machine. The frogs had left the pond and were joining in so it was all getting a bit croaky but no-one seemed to care. The tin soldiers entertained with their precision marching and the juggling clown did his best to mess them up by careering in and out of them. Lucy was really enjoying herself now. After too many hamburgers, sugary drinks and mushrooms, she sat astride the rocking horse getting very giddy and silly with the Tweenies.

The party went on. Eventually, Lucy remembered Angelina. She found her having an argument with the Bratz dolls about who the David Beckham look-alike doll fancied the most. She dragged her away before her delicate features could be damaged in a girly punch-up. Just in time as it happened, because Mr Plod the Toytown policeman turned up in Noddy's car and things could have got nasty.

As the dawn light began to creep upon them, Lucy and Angelina realised that it was nearly time for Chloe to wake up and they had been partying nearly all night.So, they said a sleepy "goodbye" to the other toys and made their way back over the garden wall, down the spider's web, up the skipping ropes and back to bed. Hopefully, Chloe's tossing and turning in the night would explain their creased clothes and messed-up hair and, with a bit of luck, Chloe's mum wouldn't come in with the vacuum cleaner and they could sleep off their hangovers.

The moral of this story, dear children, is that you don't know what your toys get up to at night. Make sure you tidy up before you go to bed, hide them all away in a box and remember, put the lid on very, very tightly.

Genre: Poetry.Topic: "Lines in the Sand". By Tony Wilson

Bournemouth in August 1921 – August 2001

Two children, friends, play hand in hand,
With sticks, draw figures in the sand.
A boy, a girl, no cares at all,
Make a castle, kick a ball.
Their parents take tea at the cliff hotel,
Play will stop with the dinner bell.

Two friends, lovers, stroll hand in hand,
Jagged lines drawn on the sand,
Barbed wire, mines, 'no entry' signs,
A grey sky heralds changing times.
The sea crashes along the shore
What will the future have in store?

Married couple walk hand in hand,
Stop, write a message in the sand.
Lasting love, celebrate with pride,
Surviving the incoming tide.
Their children skim stones, counting skips,
Laughter as one stumbles and trips.

They sit in deckchairs, hand in hand,
Picnic laid out upon the sand,
Sharing a steaming flask of tea,

Stare contentedly out to sea.
Watching seabirds, reading books,
The couple sit, sharing words, looks.

The man sits alone, stick in hand,
Her name written, lines in the sand.
Remembers life lived by the sea,
Rhythmic waves lull a memory.
While for rocks, sand and restless sea,
Life is a blink in eternity.

Genre: Non-Fiction.   Topic: "Serendipity".   By Alan Pearce
Serendipity

A "happy chance". If you think about it, both Kingdom Animalia and Kingdom Plantae mostly owe their current existence to serendipity. Evolution tells us that offspring have the characteristics of both parents, to a lesser extent grandparents, and so on, from the genes that have been passed on to them. But occasionally, very occasionally, there is a mutant gene which introduces another characteristic. Here is the important point: if this new characteristic is of hereditary value – say, a longer proboscis or a more articulate thumb, this gene will by happy chance proliferate and be passed on yet again. A brighter flower will attract more bees, a fish with bigger teeth will catch more prey, an oak which produces more acorns has a better chance of producing another offspring, a big cat which can run faster is likely to eat better during its lifetime, and so on. And over time they pass on these characteristics. Hence why predator animals have forward-facing eyes and predated animals have sideways facing eyes. And so on, again.

(It must not be forgotten, however, that there is the other kind of mutant gene. If Covid 19 mutates, we are probably in real trouble. But then, who are "we"? To human beings, "we" is "us" but to Mother Nature the correct survivors are simply the most successful species. There is no natural reason why it should be Homo Sapiens. My money is on bacteria or viruses.)

But back to serendipity as we know it. Nearly all scientific discoveries have depended upon serendipity. When Edison was told that he had not yet succeeded in inventing a light bulb and had already had 103 failures, he replied: "No, I have had 103 successes in finding different ways not to do it."

Examples of serendipity: Spencer Silver's work on adhesives, during which he discovered one that unglued and reglued itself and became the Post-it note. Fleming's penicillin cultures. Artificial sweeteners. X Rays. Pacemakers. Plunket's "Teflon". Safety matches. And Viagra – developed to treat angina, now used for another purpose. All discovered in the search for something else – serendipitous discoveries.

My friend Richard is a research scientist, an inventor, an entrepreneur. He is working on ways of producing oil from waste products and has so far succeeded in doing so from waste ice cream, out of date Marmite, and cow pats. Anything with carbon in it. But not yet in commercially viable quantities. He had to vaporise them and pass them over a sensor. A pump was necessary to achieve this. However, the sensor was so sensitive that any vibration would throw its results out. His answer was to put the pump on one table and the testing sensor on another table. Of course, they had to be connected for the vaporised gas to transfer from one to the other. He first tried a flexible steel tube, but this simply passed on the pump vibrations. So, he tried a plastic tube from a home winemakers' kit. Then a Bunsen Burner rubber tube. Still no good.

And then – serendipity. You will have to imagine for yourself the serendipitous connection, but the gentlest, softest, strongest, most pliable, malleable and tractile material yet invented was clearly the thinnest possible latex tube you could get. Where to get it from?

An idea came to him. He went to the nearest pharmacy and asked for a packet of condoms.

"Plain, or ribbed?" asked the pharmacist.

"Plain, please," said Richard.

"Do you want a decorated end or a plain end?" asked the pharmacist.

"It doesn't matter," said Richard. "I'm going to cut the end off, anyway."

Genre: Fiction.   Topic: "Retribution".   By Jan Mills

Nick's disengagement

For as long as Nick could remember Finn had always wanted what he had. No matter if it was tangible – a toy, game, book, friend, parent's attention, or more intangible – admiration, pride, approbation. If Nick had it, Finn wanted it!

Finn was fifteen months younger than Nick, who was a generous child who gladly shared whatever he had. But Finn didn't want to share; he wanted it all for himself. Their father was often away from home, leaving their mother an almost lone parent bringing up two lively boys. Finn learned early on that if he made enough of a fuss when he wanted something that Nick had, their mum would eventually say: "For heaven's sake, Nick, just give it to Finn, so we can all have some peace." And Nick would have to hand over whatever "it" was to Finn, who would smirk at him.

Finn learned he could mostly get whatever he wanted by manipulating people, and so it carried on throughout their early years and teens. When he was eighteen, Nick was glad to get into a university a couple of hundred miles from home. This was a wonderful respite from Finn, and Nick made every excuse he could think of to avoid going home for the holidays.

During his early teens Nick had some long-term, loyal friends who had resisted Finn's attempts to lure them away. Finn had been more successful at stealing some of his girlfriends. Although Nick was kinder and better-looking, Finn had a "bad boy" attitude that seemed so attractive to girls. So, when Nick met Jenny during his final year at Uni, he determined to delay introducing her to his family, and particularly Finn, for as long as possible.

Jenny was beautiful, shy, sweet-natured and everything Nick found desirable in a woman. Their relationship soon became serious and they seemed so well matched they decided to move in together after just six months. They seemed so right together that Nick proposed and Jenny accepted.

Nick wrote to his parents about his engagement, but continued to offer a string of excuses to avoid visiting his family. Then, suddenly, everything changed; his sweet and adoring girlfriend became a demanding, shrewish and nagging fiancée. Nick could not believe the transformation. The odd "tiff" became a full-blown argument, followed by a tantrum, which usually ended with something being thrown at Nick's head! He felt as if he was constantly walking on eggshells. He felt trapped, unable to extricate himself from an intolerable engagement without dire consequences to himself!

This went on for some time until, in the midst of one of Jenny's tirades, she shrieked some magic words: "…and I know you're ashamed of me because you won't even introduce me to your family..." At this point Nick stopped listening; a light bulb lit in his mind and he smiled.

Jenny was at her most shy, sweet-natured and demure best as Nick introduced her to his family. He had to admit, she looked stunning. He was extra attentive to Jenny and managed to demonstrate his affection for her at every opportunity. Jenny lapped this up – the centre of attention was her favourite place!

Nick made time, on the first evening, to have his first, and last, brother-to-brother talk with Finn. He told him how much he loved Jenny and said he could not wait for them to be married.

Nick and Jenny were staying for a full week and packed as many social activities in as they could and Nick noticed that Finn seemed to be with them nearly all the time. Jenny responded enthusiastically to all of Finn's attention. Although not handsome in the way that Nick was, Finn had a rakish charm and undefinable charisma. He and Jenny certainly seemed to get on well and were constantly talking together – conversations that stopped abruptly when Nick entered the room.

On their last evening, there was a tangible tension as they ate their last meal all together. Nick and Jenny eventually went to bed and Nick promptly fell asleep. In the morning, he woke, alone in bed. A small white envelope was propped up on his bedside table. With fingers crossed he picked up the envelope and slit it open. As he read, he began to smile – a smile that widened into a huge grin as he read on…

"Dear Nick

I know this will come as terrible shock, but I cannot marry you. I know this will devastate you, but Finn and I cannot deny the way we feel about each other and we know we are meant to be together..."

The engagement ring fell to the floor and Nick's grin dissolved into laughter. Oh yes! Jenny and Finn were meant to be together; they certainly deserved each other!

Retribution indeed!

Genre: Non-fiction. Topic: "Wonder". By Lesley Watts

Sargent at the Tate

Once through the hallowed porticoes and into the resplendent vaulted ceilings of the entrance at Tate Britain, you are immediately drawn into a bygone era of opulence and wealth ... of light and space ... of calm. Past the spiral staircase leading down to the Whistler room and café – where there is an apologist's film lambasting Rex Whistler for his portrayal of slaves as monkeys, rightly so, but conversely failing to recognise his skill and vision in an otherwise beautiful mural ... and in so doing seeming to cleverly deflect attention away from the Tate's family connections and their benefitting from that abhorrent trade of that time!

But I digress ... beyond the staircase, past Renaissance art, the permanent JMW Turner and Constable exhibitions, the Henry Moore and Elisabeth Frisk sculptures, you arrive at the John Singer Sargent exhibition rooms, where you're immediately immersed into the colour, elegance and extravagance of the late 19th to early 20th centuries.

Interspersed with the works of art are some of the fashion and accessories Sargent's sitters wore at the time. The colour, material, detail and style of those alone are exquisite and breathtaking; the elegance of the era embodied in those glass cases.

In one instance there is a portrait of a Spanish dancer in beads and glorious gold fabric with a full skirt, embellished and exotic. Alongside is the original costume, allowing you to admire and study the detail; then on the other side of the portrait is a black and white, grainy film of the dancer and dress in beautiful, fluid movement. A feast for the senses.

Sargent is purported to have worked with his sitters to choose the right clothing, usually their own, as well as choosing the sitter's pose, the lighting, setting and expression; even going so far as to pin the clothing a certain way to get the correct fall and folds of materials he desired. Almost like a modern-day fashion photographic shoot.

To quote: "Sargent used fashion as a powerful tool to express identity and personality. He regularly chose the outfits of his collaborators or manipulated their clothing."

Some have simple backdrops, and others are more involved. One of a lady slightly reclining, sitting at a piano with one arm over the back of her chair and her other hand gently resting on the keyboard, is breathtaking. Another of two children surrounded by lilies, holding lanterns – their gazes on the task at hand and not the artist – is enchanting. And a third of a lady in evening dress, in profile with her hand on a simple wooden table is simple and beautiful. Because these paintings are so well staged there is a sense of the theatrical, no more so than the actress Ellen Terry as Lady Macbeth who is stunning with long, braided red hair wearing a deep green Shakespearean dress with wide sleeves, standing with crown poised above her head.

The personalities of the sitters' shine through. Sargent manages to capture the relaxed expressions of his subjects, which draws the viewers' eyes. A mischievous glint in an expression, a slightly upturned mouth all add to the connection. His portrayals of hands also feel proportional and real. An artist very much in tune with the human form. Most capture the full length of the sitters, sitting or standing, and a few mirror the old masters' three-quarter length vision.

Rather than the usual paintings of the aristocracy or 'old' money of the time, instead he favoured commissions from socialites and 'new' money reflecting the emergent American industrial age and importance on a growing worldwide stage. His close association and friendship with the Sassoon family is celebrated in several paintings.

And, whilst most of the art on display celebrates the female form there are also three magnificent paintings of men – two in full medals and regalia, and one of a doctor in a full-length red robe. These are equally remarkable.

This exhibition is a successful celebration of an artist who is able to capture and immortalise a period of time with empathy and a skilled eye. His mastery of colour and form engages and delights the audience with his reflection and commentary on the era it encapsulates.

Genre: Fiction". Topic: "Danger". By Carol Waterkeyn

Moment of glory

Choirmaster Greg made an announcement. Another member of the choir had gone. This time, Kate. It meant there would be fewer of them for the annual

Christmas concert in St Mary's Hall. A murmur went around the choir. Bridget looked at Greg and shrugged sympathetically.

The numbers had been diminishing, especially among the sopranos. With Kate and her stroke, and Sarah recently passing after a heart attack, Bridget knew the soprano section of the choir had really suffered.

So, Bridget said she would be delighted to step up and join the lead group. Greg had asked her after the rehearsal that evening, and Bridget was ecstatic. She liked Greg a lot and hoped he would soon choose her as first soprano for the Christmas-themed pieces they were rehearsing. Walking home afterwards with Alison, one of the altos, she could hardly contain her excitement.

"Well done," said Alison. "It's a terrible shame about Sarah, though. She had such a beautiful voice and I will miss her."

"Well, of course, we all will," said Bridget, looking at her feet.

"It was a real shock about Kate as well," continued Alison with a frown, "I mean she's quite young to have a stroke, don't you think? It's so sad, she can hardly talk now, let alone sing."

"I know," was all Bridget could think of to say. As they reached her street, Bridget turned to her fellow choir member. "Well, see you next week, Alison."

"Yes. See you then." Alison waved as she turned the corner.

Bridget opened her front door and, when she was safely inside her terraced cottage, punched the air. "Yes!"

Adeline the cat came to greet her and meowed a welcome.

"Hello puss'cat. We're celebrating. I'll open a can of salmon for us both for supper this evening."

Bridget stroked the cat's soft dark fur, and it followed her into the kitchen, sensing dinner time.

After their meal, Bridget rang her elderly father in the nursing home.

"You'll never guess what, Dad, I think I am going to be lead soprano at the concert. A few people have left recently, so I'm really hopeful."

"That's all well and good, Bridget but remember, you shouldn't count your chickens …"

"I know. Anyway, are you okay?"

Her father proceeded to tell her today's list of complaints about the staff at the home, which always made Bridget depressed. She tried to remain cheerful, but it was hard when her father was so negative. She ended the call as soon as she was able to. Maybe she needed to do something about her father.

Bridget went to her wardrobe and pulled out a box of fabric remnants and sewing items. She removed the top layer of fabric and nestled below were the cloth dolls she had been making. The recent ones she had created were little Kate with her long blonde hair made out of yellow wool, and one of Sarah with her brown curly hair. Both had a large pin stuck in them. Maybe she should make one for her father with his bald patch and cruel mouth. Yes, maybe it was time.

Bridget couldn't wait to get to the next choir meeting. There were only two weeks of rehearsals till the concert. She was a bit later arriving than she would have liked. She'd been delayed by her father's nursing home ringing to say the old man had taken a turn for the worse but they were keeping a close eye on him. Consequently, she was a bit flustered entering the rehearsal room at the village hall. Greg was already speaking to the choir:

"…and so, I have brought in reinforcements; well, one to be precise." He smiled. "This is my younger sister Emily. She sings with the University

Choir and has kindly agreed to step in and take the soprano solos."

A tall, elegant young woman walked forward and raised her hand in greeting.

"Hello everyone, it's super to be here."

Bridget seethed. She was going to have to conjure up some more magic and make another doll when she got home. It was going to need more material this time and, a smaller pin through the throat to last for the next two weeks at least. She didn't want Emily to die, because she didn't want to upset the lovely Greg, but she needed his sister out of the way if Bridget was, at last, to have her moment of glory.

Genre: Fact-based story.   Topic: "Danger".   By Barbara Shea

Coming back from France

The small French sailing boat rose and fell gently in the dark water just outside Lyme Regis harbour. William had never known a night so still or with so many bright stars. He took out his pocket watch and in the bright full moonlight could see that it was nearly midnight. Just a few more hours until dawn, when the carriage would arrive. He felt a thrill of excitement at the thought of returning to his homeland, tempered by the fear of being caught and arrested once again. If that happened, he knew there would be no escape. The charge of sodomy in the year of 1841 was a grave one and a vindictive judge could sentence him to a lengthy term of imprisonment, or even invoke the death penalty. It was certainly amongst the many sexual peccadilloes which would not be tolerated either in England, nor in his adoptive Italy.

He pushed these thoughts from his mind and settled down for a long wait. A cabin boy appeared with bread, cold beef and a hot toddy of rum. Gradually the sky lightened, and eventually he made out the hooded figure of his trusted servant John approaching from the shore in a small rowing boat. Neither of them spoke as he was rowed towards the sand and shingle beach, or as he stepped delicately from the boat, taking care not to get sea water on his buckled shoes or his fine silk stockings. He was a fastidious man, and the fact that he had fled his homeland and had to return secretly had not altered this. It would not do for a servant to see the owner of Kingston Lacy, one of the grandest houses in Dorset, in a dishevelled state.

Once in the carriage, he reflected on the way his life had turned out. He had always been an adventurer, always courted danger, but the liaison with a Guardsman in London had been a step too far and despite being fully aware of where his actions might lead, it was in his nature to believe he was invincible. Events had proved otherwise.

He must have dozed, as the next thing he was aware of was the carriage rumbling to a halt. The front door of Kingston Lacy House opened quickly, he stepped inside and the door immediately closed behind him.

His brother George was there, shaking his hand and looking slightly exasperated, as he usually did during these dangerous visits. After all, if William were to be caught, he would also end up before the magistrate for harbouring a criminal. Poor George. As William's younger brother, he had been left with the task of administering the grand house when William had decided to flee England rather than face the court. Even while abroad, William was a hard task master, frequently sending back various treasures acquired in Italy and France together with lengthy letters and copious notes on the placement of these within the house. No wonder George always looked nervous and harassed during these visits!

With the exception of the elderly and trusted housekeeper, all the servants had been given the day off in an effort to minimise the danger of an arrest. The servants, of course, found the offer of a day off strange and completely out of the usual order of things, but on pain of instant dismissal if they speculated on this to anyone, they kept their suspicions to themselves and were just grateful for the unexpected holiday.

William wandered at a leisurely pace from room to room, noting where his latest acquisitions had been placed and tutting at those which had not been displayed to his satisfaction, brother George following quietly behind. However, when they came to the double oak doors he had bought from the Vatican, with the Fleur de Lys carved in the centre and now placed at the far side of the Saloon, even he was stunned by their magnificence, and at least had the good grace to say so, much to George's relief.

All too soon, or at least as far as William was concerned, the carriage once again was at the door and William and George said their hasty goodbyes. Neither knew when, or even if, they would see each other again and despite the dangerous and exacting nature of William's infrequent visits, the brotherly bond was still strong.

The carriage ride back to Lyme Regis, the boat journey back to France and the subsequent horse ride through France and then carriage to Italy was as uneventful as they were likely to be in those days. Once home in Venice, he embarked on further purchases of treasures for Kingston Lacy in the hope of returning to live there at some point in the future. He never did.

Genre: Fiction.   Topic: "Retribution".   By Tony Wilson

The anniversary appearance

I have been to Cornwall many times on summer holidays but this was my first time out of season. I was sent by my employers to evaluate the viability of doing business in the area and was staying in Penzance. Having concluded this task a little earlier than expected and finding myself with a half day on my hands, I decided to drive down to Land's End before returning to my hotel to spend my last evening typing up my report.

Land's End proved as rugged and exciting as I expected, but with the weather closing in, I decided to make my way back to Penzance – but on the coastal road this time. I realised, however, after about a mile, that I may have made a mistake, as sea fog drifted rapidly inland. I soon found myself unable to see more than a few feet in front of my windscreen. As I reckoned, I was only a matter of a few yards from the cliff edge; you can imagine my anxiety about this being a one-way trip to Davy Jones' locker. I opened my window to try and gain extra visibility but it made little difference, so I stopped at the next signpost to see if I could find a turn-off inland.

Opening my glove compartment, I found a torch and stepped out of the car. I was about to investigate the sign when a sound caught my attention. I strained to listen, and thought I heard shouting coming from the sea. Using the light from my torch I lit the ground in front of me and through the worsening gloom I gingerly made my way to the cliff edge. I was upon the rim of land horrifyingly quickly. There through the patchy fog I saw the shape of a three-masted schooner floundering on the jagged rocks, and the sickening sound of breaking timbers mixed with the frantic, desperate noise of the souls onboard trying to save themselves from certain death.

As I looked away from this awful vision, I noticed on an outcrop of rock below and to my left, two shadowy figures. They were both men, dressed in tricorn hats, frockcoats and thigh-high riding boots. One man held aloft a lantern. Their faces seemed to be set on the unfortunate vessel in the churning waters.

Not sure what to do, I called out to them, but getting no response I carefully made my way back to my car to raise the alarm at the first house I could find.

Trying to come to terms with what I had just witnessed, I drove on until I saw a building, its windows lit, emerging from the fog. It was an inn. The sign said:"The Retribution". I parked up and quickly entered the bar room. I was the only patron, and I approached the barman and asked for a whiskey. I was about to add that I needed to use the telephone and summon the coastguard, when I caught sight of a large painting on the wall above the fireplace. It was the stricken ship I had just seen being wrecked. I walked as if in a trance to study it, and read the legend below it. It read: "The Retribution, sunk with all hands 1780, the victim of wreckers."

The barman brought my drink over, and broke the silence. "This pub is named after the ship. She went down on this night exactly two hundred years ago. It was foggy then, too, apparently. Terrible business."

Genre: Fact based story.   Topic: "Surprise."   By Alan Pearce

Happy endings

Messrs. Swarbrick and Hutton of Alderholt, Dorset, was a light engineering company in the 1960s. It was a family-run company with very loyal and long-serving staff. It had been going for years. Many of the staff had been with them for the same number of years.

Alf Froud was foreman of the cast iron section. But, of course, the foremen of all six sections stood in for each other from time to time, such as holidays, because they all had sufficient knowledge broadly, as well as deep knowledge of their own specifically. Alf was a worried man, however. The writing was on the wall for the cast iron department because so many things were now made of tough plastic and were much cheaper. The directors were worried men, too. Compensation for the demise of the cast iron section required mere tweaking of the overall operation, but what were they going to do with Alf? He'd been with them longest of all – they couldn't just lay him off; it would break his heart and be the end of him. And his voluntary Youth Training programme would surely suffer, too.

As D-Day approached they brought in a firm of management consultants. Sadly, their only conclusion was to lay Alf off. But then a junior member of the consultant company had a "blue sky", "out of the box" thought. He said "I couldn't help noticing that your receptionist is pregnant. Can you tell me what her intentions are?"

Swarbrick was plussed. "What do you want to know that for?" he asked. "But if you must know, she's made it quite clear that she's going to take her maternity leave and then not come back. She has effectively resigned. We shall miss her, too."

"Okay," said the tyro, "make Alf your receptionist."

"Are you out of your mind?" said almost everybody, along with remarks about long legs and short skirts.

"No," he replied, "Alf knows nearly everything there is to know about this company and its products. Most of the receptionist's work is on the 'phone, anyway. Just give it a try."

In the face of the alternative, both Swarbrick and Hutton and the other consultants agreed to a three-month trial, which would also give Alf time to see how he felt about it.

It was done. At first, nothing happened. Then one day a highly stressed manufacturer rang to say that the pressure release valve on his Clarkson converter had failed yet again and could he purchase a replacement?

Alf, the new receptionist, said: "Before you replace it, have you wondered why it keeps failing? What's the model you've got made of?"

The reply was: "steel."

And Alf said: "That's it, then. I happen to know that the Clarkson converter access ports on all the new models is ali. You've got bimetal corrosion and if you replace it, it's going to get worse and then go on happening."

"Oh," said the caller. "What should I do? It's urgent – we're losing money."

Alf replied: "You need an interstitial washer and a replaceable copper filter, together with a moulded shroud. There's a new combo on the market. It's slightly more expensive, but they last forever. I could have it with you first thing in the morning if you wish."

The caller did wish. He was so grateful that he wrote personally to Swarbrick to compliment him on Alf's knowledge and the help he had received.

Then another telephone call: "I need some 6inch by ¾ No8 mild steel bolts but I can't find them on the web because they're Whitworth."

"We've tested carefully and found that if you drill out just one mill, then a 20mm bolt will be just as good. Any 20mm bolt. We have them in stock – they aren't expensive."

And another: "I have a J4 Mod.3 attenuator. My 200-psi charger keeps making it cut out."

"You don't need 200 psi for that Mod. Simply readjust it to 150. You don't need to change anything else, or buy anything."

"Are you the receptionist?"

"Yes."

Two years later, Swarbrick and Hutton put Alf up for a community MBE and Her Majesty was graciously pleased to award it.

Genre: Non-fiction.Careful use of correct language: A big cock-up! (By Anon)

Proper use of language

Swansea Council had built a new office block, with its own car park. It was in the centre of Swansea. The car park was a very attractive site for drivers, and was misused. The Council decided to put up a notice: "Private parking for Swansea Council employees only. Unauthorised vehicles will be clamped and owner fined."

Welsh law says that notices and signs have to be in Welsh as well as English. Swansea did not have a Welsh speaker.

Cardiff Council had a Welsh Interpreter. His services were available to other councils, online.

Swansea Council sent an e-mail to Cardiff asking for their car-parking sign to be translated into Welsh.

The answer came back very quickly. Swansea had a huge sign made immediately, in both languages, and erected at once.

It said, at the top, in English, "Private parking for Swansea Council employees only. Unauthorised vehicles will be clamped and owner fined."

Underneath, in Welsh, this huge sign said: "I am away from the office at the moment. Please send your script in a separate text and I will translate it and return it to you as soon as possible."

Not a problem we have in Verwood!

Printed in Great Britain
by Amazon